Praise for the Raine Stockton Dog Mystery Series

"An exciting, original and suspense-laden whodunit... A simply fabulous mystery starring a likeable, dedicated heroine..."
--*Midwest Book Review*

"A delightful protagonist...a well-crafted mystery."
--*Romantic Times*

"There can't be too many golden retrievers in mystery fiction for my taste."
--*Deadly Pleasures*

" An intriguing heroine, a twisty tale, a riveting finale, and a golden retriever to die for. [This book] will delight mystery fans and enchant dog lovers."
---*Carolyn Hart*

"Has everything--wonderful characters, surprising twists, great dialogue. Donna Ball knows dogs, knows the Smoky Mountains, and knows how to write a page turner. I loved it."
--*Beverly Connor*

"Very entertaining… combines a likeable heroine and a fascinating mystery… a story of suspense with humor and tenderness."

--*Carlene Thompson*

SILENT NI

A Raine Stockton D

Donna B

www.donnaball.net

Published by Blue Merle Publishing
Drawer H
Mountain City Georgia 30562

ISBN-13: 978-0977329625
ISBN-10: 0977329623

This book is also available in digital format for your e-reader.

First Printing November 2011

This book is for the magnificent Tsaligi Dakota Legend, CGC,VC, HIC, BPD, OJC, NTC, W-TFD/MF, W-FD/MF/HTM, Registered Therapy Dog.

You changed lives. Can anyone ask for more?

12/14/99—7/28/11

ONE

Ashleigh had just finished hanging the string of Christmas lights over the front door when she saw the flash of lights round the corner of Willow Lane, and Dusty Harper's red pickup truck pulled up in front of the trailer. Her daddy had lost his license a year ago and sometimes Dusty would run into him at the Last Chance Bar & Grille and give him a ride home. Ashleigh's stomach always knotted up when she heard Dusty's pickup truck chugging around the corner because she knew that meant they'd both been drinking. Nothing good ever happened when the two of them went out drinking.

She hurried to drag the kitchen chair on which she had been standing back inside just as the truck door opened and her daddy spilled out, cussing loudly for no good reason at all. Dusty yelled back at him to shut the eff up and mind his own effing business, and Ashleigh shut the door quickly so she couldn't hear any more. She hated it when her daddy and his drinking buddies stood in the yard throwing F-bombs, not because she was such a prude, but because their neighbor, 62-year-old Leona Silva, had already called the cops on them twice this year. Fine for her, but when the squad car pulled away Ashleigh was the one alone in the trailer with an angry drunk. Just thinking about it made her feel sick to her stomach again with dread.

Although she couldn't hear the words, she could still hear them out there arguing as she hurried around the room straightening up the mess: a couple of empty cardboard boxes the Christmas ornaments had come in, some stray tinsel, the strands of lights she hadn't had a chance to untangle yet. Maybe if she hid the clutter he wouldn't notice the four-foot plastic tree she'd decorated in the corner, or the Nativity scene she'd set up on the dinette set, and if he didn't notice, he wouldn't have any reason to yell at her.

Why a Christmas tree would make him mad, she didn't know, and it didn't matter. When Daddy was drunk, he didn't need a reason to get mad.

She heard the engine of the pickup truck roar, and gravel sputtered as Dusty drove off. A few seconds later the front door burst open and her daddy stood there, red-eyed and glaring.

"What is all this crap?" He grabbed the Christmas lights that wreathed the door—which she had forgotten to unplug—and jerked them down. "Ain't you got nothing better to do than trash this place up like a whorehouse? Answer me, girl!"

He kicked the door shut and came toward her with a strand of lights knotted in his hand, but she stood her ground.

"I was just trying to pretty the place up a little for Christmas," she said. "Mama always did."

"Don't you talk to me about your mama!" He threw the lights at her, and she couldn't help flinching, even though it didn't come close to hitting her. "You see your *mama* any place around here? Electricity costs money, girl!"

She bent down to pick up the lights. "Yes, sir."

He shoved past her and into the narrow kitchen, and every muscle in her body tensed as he flung open the refrigerator door and she realized she had forgotten to check to see if there was any beer. *Please, please, please…*

She heard the clink of a bottle and relaxed marginally as he pushed past her again, beer in hand. She held her breath until he got past the Christmas tree without noticing it and sat down heavily in the vinyl recliner. In a moment he grunted, "Anything to eat?"

"Some ham left over from last night," she offered quickly. "You want me to make you a sandwich?"

"The way you eat, I'm surprised there's anything left at all. Nobody likes a fatty."

He tilted the beer bottle to his mouth and picked up the remote control. ESPN blared to life on the 30-

inch flat screen he'd bought when he'd still had a job down at the plant. He used to drink a lot back then, too—in fact he'd been drinking most of Ashleigh's fourteen years or at least the ones she could remember—but he hadn't started getting mean about it until the plant laid him off.

He said, "Don't put no mustard on it."

She took out the plate of ham and a butcher knife and that was when the phone rang. She snatched up the kitchen extension, hoping he wouldn't hear the ring over the television, and tried to sink back against the opposite wall where her father couldn't see if he happened to glance over his shoulder.

"Hello?" Her voice was breathless, muffled by the hand she held close to the receiver.

"Hey." It was Nick, just as she had feared. "You want me to come over or what?"

"I told you not to call this late." She edged back further into the corner, her voice low as she darted another anxious glance toward the living room. "I'm going to get in trouble."

"That better not be that worthless boy calling up this time of night," her father yelled. "You tell him he comes sniffing around here I'll whip his ass!"

Ashleigh's eyes flew in alarm to the living room, where her daddy was lurching up from the recliner. "I've got to go," she said urgently. "Don't call back. I'll see you after school tomorrow."

"Hey—"

She turned to hang up the phone but as she did the cord, which was stretched across the kitchen table, caught the edge of the platter and sent the ham crashing to the floor.

"Look what you did, you stupid cow!"

The beer bottle sailed past her shoulder and shattered against the wall behind her. She dropped to her knees and scrambled to pick up the spilled ham. The telephone receiver hit the floor but she could hear Nick saying, "You still there? Hey, you still there?" And then her daddy's boot slammed the receiver across the floor and she didn't hear anything else from it.

Ashleigh got to her feet with her hands full of the greasy ham, and her daddy lunged toward her, his face like thunder. "You expect me to eat that? You fixing to feed me food that's been on the floor, is that what you're gonna do?"

"Daddy, I can wash it off. It's not that dirty, see? It won't take but a minute—"

He drew back his arm and knocked the ham out of her hands. And while she stared, stunned and afraid, at the mess on the floor, he drew back his arm again. That was when she snatched up the butcher knife that was still lying on the table.

"Don't do it," she said, but her eyes were pleading as she backed a step away. "Daddy, don't."

But he just looked at the way she held the knife, two-handed and weak-wristed in front of her, and his eyes glinted with scorn, and he just kept coming.

TWO

I'm pretty sure Norman Rockwell never even heard of Hanover County, North Carolina, or of Hansonville, the county seat and my home town. But if he had, he probably would have painted it, because we still know how to do Christmas right. Every street lamp is wrapped with greenery and red bows. There's a wreath on every shop window, twinkling lights around every doorway, and a huge reindeer-drawn sleigh atop the roof of Hanson's Department store. There are fake snowmen on the lawn of City Hall and the walkway to the courthouse is lined with Christmas trees all decked out in red bows and multicolored Christmas lights. A huge spruce tree sits in the town square, and the ceremonial lighting of the tree each year rivals anything Rockefeller Center has to offer. And even though we don't generally get snow until the middle of January, no one ever seems to get tired of hearing "White Christmas" on the radio.

My name is Raine Stockton. I live here in the mountains of western North Carolina with my gorgeous dogs: two Australian shepherds, Mischief and Magic, and my golden retriever, Cisco. My beautiful collie, Majesty, is currently living with my Aunt Mart, who had a difficult time adjusting to Uncle Roe's heart attack and subsequent retirement a few months back. Having Majesty around has been the best thing that could have happened to her, and I've never seen Majesty happier, but make no mistake about it—Majesty is still my dog.

Up until the so-called downturn in the economy—which around here is more like a full-blown depression—I worked part time for the Forest Service and ran a full-time boarding kennel and training facility with my business partner, Maude. Now it doesn't look as though the Forest Service will be able to afford me even part-time when the tourist season starts again, and my kennel has been closed for remodeling since October. The closest thing I have to a full-time job these days is volunteering with Cisco in search and rescue, our therapy dog work, or whatever we can find to keep us busy. And even without a job, Christmas is my busiest time of the year.

It was Friday, two weeks before Christmas, and Cisco, wearing a fur-trimmed Santa hat and a big red velvet bow, patiently posed for his eighty-seventh photo of the day. Christmas with Santa Dog was the highlight of Hansonville Elementary and Middle School's holiday season and has been the undoing of more than one underpaid elementary grade teacher, not to mention her well-meaning, elf-clad temporary assistant... me.

To be absolutely honest, I don't think anyone has actually died due to Santa Dog, but I can't help but notice the rate of attrition in third-grade teachers is unusually high, particularly during the holidays. So far the damage had been fairly light: Cisco toppled over the Christmas tree in his rush to take a bite out of the gingerbread house; Lincoln White had tried to feed Santa Dog a chocolate bar and, when I averted that disaster, he had threatened a temper tantrum unless allowed to share his cherry punch with Cisco, who happily overturned the cup onto Lincoln's white shirt. Lincoln thought that was hilarious, but I had a feeling I'd be hearing from his parents. Kitty Rogers threw up red-and-green frosting in the cardboard cut-out sleigh, and only a quick grab of Cisco's collar prevented an embarrassing– and disgusting– incident. After that, Mrs. Holloway turned kind of greenish and seemed to lose her holiday spirit. I knew how she felt. In four and a half yards of green elf felt with bells jingling from every appendage, I was swimming in sweat, sick of the smell of sugar, and ready to go home.

On the positive side, though, the kids were having a great time.

When the last snapshot was taken and the last cupcake eaten, Cisco was presented with his ritual basket of dog biscuits wrapped in red cellophane with a sloppy green bow. Cubbies were cleaned out, coats buttoned up, and the final bell before the winter holidays dismissed a stream of squealing third-graders into the hallway, trailing Christmas ribbons and glitter posters and waving their photos of Santa Dog. I felt sorry for Cisco in all the noise and confusion, and stayed to chat with Mrs. Holloway only long enough for the corridors to clear out. Cisco loves kids and, except for one or two minor incidents, had been a perfect guest. But I didn't want to push my luck and we still had one more stop to make today. I left him in a down-stay by the door while I helped the teacher clean up the room.

"Are you and Cisco going to be in the Christmas parade tonight?" asked Mrs. Holloway as we went around the room, raking leftover paper plates, cups and wrapping paper into a big black trash bag.

Ruth Holloway was actually a few years younger than I was, with bouncy blond curls and a cherubic face that made her look even younger. But I had been calling her "Mrs. Holloway" for the past five years that I had been bringing therapy dogs to her class, and I just couldn't get comfortable calling her by her first name — in the same way it's hard to call your pastor or your doctor by his first name. So I generally tried to avoid the problem by not using her name at all.

"I'm giving Cisco the night off," I told her. "My friend Sonny is loaning some of her sheep and her border collie for the parade and the living Nativity afterwards, and I promised to help her." Mystery, Sonny's border collie, was a brilliant working dog, but

Sonny's limited mobility made it difficult for her to walk in the parade.

"Oh, that's right, we're having real sheep this year!" Ruth flashed me a quick brilliant smile as she knotted the drawstrings on the trash bag. "I'm playing Mary in the Nativity the next two weekends," she added, "and my husband, Jack, is playing Joseph."

That was perfect casting, as anyone who knew the Holloways would agree. Ruth was one of those genuinely nice people who never turned down a request or left a need unmet; she was a Brownie leader, head of the March of Dimes, and volunteered at the food bank twice a week. Her husband was the youth pastor at the Methodist church, a volunteer firefighter, and a Little League coach. They went on mission trips, hosted foreign exchange students, and were one of the few qualified foster homes for troubled and disadvantaged children in a county that was desperately in need of foster homes.

But even as she spoke, a kind of wistful expression came over her face and she added, "Maybe it will bring us luck, if that's not too awful to say. We've been trying to get pregnant for two years."

"Oh." I never knew how to respond to things like that. "Well, you never know, I guess."

She smiled a little apologetically. "I guess that was tactless of me. I heard about you and Buck. I'm sorry."

Buck Lawson, my on-again,off-again husband of over ten years, and I had finally untied the knot for good recently. I was fine with it, really. I mean, it was inevitable and the best thing for both of us. As long as I didn't spend too much time thinking about the fact that for the first Christmas I could remember Buck would be sitting at someone else's table...well, it was fine. Really.

I said, "Thanks. But it's fine. Really."

She hurried on, the way people usually do, "Anyway, we're excited about being in the Nativity." She dropped a wadded-up napkin filled with something gooey into the trash bag and moved to the next desk. "My neighbors, the Wilkins, are donating their donkey, and Sadie Tompkins is bringing llamas— I think they're supposed to be camels, but when they're all dressed up in those fancy saddles, who can tell, right?"

I grinned in agreement. "It sounds like it's going to be really something. The best Nativity this town has ever had, anyway. Don't worry about the sheep," I added, "they do whatever Mystery tells them to. Sonny will be there every night, but Mystery is the one who really does the work."

"Well, if Mystery is half as smart as Cisco," said Mrs. Holloway, with a fond glance toward my Golden, "those sheep are in good hands."

Cisco raised his ears expectantly when he heard his name, then dropped them again when no treat was forthcoming. I tried not to look too reluctant as I glanced around the room with its miles of red and green crepe paper, the Christmas tree and cardboard sleigh, the general messiness of everything and offered tentatively, "Is there anything else I can do to help?"

She laughed and made a shooing gesture. "Go on, get out of here. I get paid for this—kind of—and you and Cisco have done your share. Thank you," she added sincerely. "For some of these kids, this was the best part of Christmas."

And it was words like that that made what we did worth every minute.

I said my goodbyes and made my way to the girl's restroom to change.

The Hansonville Elementary and Middle School temporarily accommodated grades one through nine while the School Board waited for funding to complete construction on the new middle school building across the street. The younger grades were confined to the west wing of the building, and grades six through nine to the east, with the gym and cafeteria in the middle. The restrooms on the west side of the building were far too crowded with squealing little girls for me to try to squeeze in with Cisco, so we hurried through the gym to the bathrooms on the middle school side.

If you have never tried to change out of an elf costume in a bathroom stall with a seventy-pound golden retriever at your side, you have missed out on one of life's greatest adventures. It becomes even more challenging when said golden retriever knows perfectly well there is a basket of dog biscuits with his name on it in the tote bag at his feet. I managed to wiggle out of the green felt and into my jeans while keeping Cisco's nose out of the tote and pulled on a festive Christmas-themed sweater embroidered with golden retriever puppies wearing red bows and, yes, jingle bells across the front. Our next stop was the nursing home, and the residents loved holiday-themed sweaters almost as much as they loved Cisco.

Standing on one foot and using Cisco for balance, I was pulling on my boot when I heard the bathroom door open. I quickly grabbed Cisco's collar so that he wouldn't scoot under the door to greet the newcomer, overbalanced, and almost landed in the toilet. Trying not to swear—there were children and dogs present, after all—I pulled Cisco away from the stall door and the tote bag and stuffed my other foot into its boot. That was when I heard the sobbing.

I have a confession to make. I'm not very good with kids. I don't find them very interesting, I never know what to say to them, and the only time I'm even marginally comfortable around them is when Cisco is there to act as a grinning, wiggling buffer between us. So when I heard crying in the bathroom, I grimaced visibly and took my time opening the stall door, hoping that whoever it was would either pull herself together or go away before I came out.

She didn't.

I opened the door a crack and peeked out, expecting a little girl who was brokenhearted over an imagined slight by her BFF or because she'd gotten the cheap box of peppermints in the class gift exchange. But then I heard her say in a high, shaky, gasping voice, "Nick? You've got to come get me, Nick, something terrible has happened. I need your help...Can't you borrow your brother's car? No, I can't do that! You said... I know but you said..."

I stepped out of the stall tentatively, keeping Cisco on a short leash. The girl who was hunched over the sink was clearly in one of the upper grades, tall and broadly built—well, ok, plump—in worn jeans and a big shirt that did nothing to minimize her figure problems. Her dark hair was dull and tangled-looking as it fell around her shoulders, and her face was pale and blotched with crying. She whirled around when she heard us, a stricken look on her face, and disconnected the phone.

I tried for a smile that was both casual and concerned, but that did not look too threatening or adult.

"Are you okay?"

Her eyes dropped to Cisco, who, even without his Santa Dog hat, could not have looked more adorable. He grinned and swished his tail and pulled a little against the leash, eager to make a new friend. I reminded him, "With me," and he settled down.

She looked quickly away from Cisco when I spoke and swiped an unsteady hand over her face, half turning and avoiding my eyes. She said, "I'm fine." But her voice sounded thick and tight and as shaky as she looked. I thought she might actually be coming down with something.

I was careful to keep my distance as I offered, "Because I can get a teacher or something if you…"

The door opened and another girl of about the same age pushed in, bringing with her a brief burst of noise from the corridor. "Hey, you about finished with my phone? Oh! Look at the dog!"

She rushed over to us and started petting Cisco, and the first girl thrust the cell phone at her and hurried out. By the time I disentangled Cisco from what quickly became a half dozen giggling, cooing middle-grade girls who wanted to tell me all about their own dogs, we were fifteen minutes late for our next therapy dog visit, and I had all but forgotten about the teenager weeping on the phone.

THREE

Nursing homes are generally not the most cheerful places in the world, but with a Christmas tree in the lobby and blinking reindeer antlers on the volunteers' heads, even the antiseptic-smelling, linoleum-tiled facility managed to take on a festive air. One of the church groups had sent Christmas cards to all of the residents, and the Women's Club decorated the doors every year with artificial wreaths, so even the wheelchair-lined halls looked less bleak than they usually did. The Christmas cards were taped around the doorframes and the beribboned wreaths had candy canes on them. Cisco, prancing down the hall with his red velvet jingle-bell bow sounding merrily and his tail swishing back and forth, managed to dislodge about half a dozen Christmas cards, which slowed our progress considerably as I continually had to stop and tape them back on the doorframes.

The mobile patients—mobile in this case meaning those who were able to sit up in a wheelchair—were assembled in the cafeteria, where there was a tabletop Christmas tree in one corner and a festoon of red and green construction paper cutouts strung around the walls. The room had that odd institution-food smell that was a mixture of canned green beans, warmed-over dinner rolls, and tomato sauce. It was, of course, one of Cisco's favorite rooms in the world.

Cafeteria chairs had been arranged in a semicircle around the room for those without wheelchairs, and there were perhaps twenty-five elderly and disabled people there waiting for us. They could hear the bells on Cisco's collar coming down the hall, and by the time we entered, hands were reaching and faces were beaming. Cisco sat before each and every chair in turn, offering his paw for a handshake, grinning and basking in the affection.

Mr. Morrissey told me about his cocker spaniel, as he always did, and tried to sneak Cisco a piece of fried chicken that he had saved from lunch, as he always did. Mrs. Daniels, who had been a hairdresser for forty-five years, wanted to brush Cisco's coat, so I always carried his soft-bristle brush with me. The nurses told me that Mrs. Daniels consistently had more flexibility in her hands after grooming Cisco, and he loved it. I made small talk as I moved down the line, but I knew the one they had really come here to see was Cisco. My feelings were not hurt when they ignored me and fawned over Cisco. In fact, my feelings would have been hurt if they had not.

I tried to spend an equal amount of time with each patient, but I have to admit I enjoyed visiting with some people more than others. I always saved Esther Kelp for last because she was, quite simply, one of the most interesting people I had ever known. She had been a makeup artist in Hollywood during the fifties and sixties, in the days of the Big Studios. She had known Ronald Regan and Montgomery Cliff. She had worked on movies like *Breakfast at Tiffany's* and *Giant.* She knew Frances Bavier (remember Aunt Bea from *The Andy Griffith Show*?) which is a huge deal here in North Carolina. But even more impressive than that was the fact that *she had actually known Lassie.* She used to have lunch with Rudd Weatherwax, who, I hardly need explain, was Lassie's owner/trainer and a legend in the world of dogs. Eventually she married a man from Raleigh, and they retired here in the mountains. She had the best stories of anyone I had ever known. And she was the only person in the world who could beat me at Lassie trivia.

"Well, hello there, Mr. Cisco!" She greeted my dog, beaming. "Don't you look like Christmas come uptown?"

Cisco sat and swept his tail across the floor, smiling his biggest smile, as I bent to hug Miss Esther. She was a petite woman, all bone and sinew, with crisp silver curls and clear hazel eyes. She was always impeccably groomed, and today she wore a pale pink velour track suit with pearl earrings and carefully applied makeup. She had broken her hip in a fall from a ladder while painting the trim on her house back in the beginning of autumn, complications had set in, and since she had no one to take care of her at home, she had been sent here from the hospital to recuperate. She had graduated from the walker to a four-pronged cane over the past month and looked fitter than most people I saw on the street.

"I thought they would have kicked you out of this place by now," I told her with a grin.

Her eyes twinkled. "Bah! They can't get rid of me. But there is some news. My grandson in California is fixing up his guest house and he won't have anything but that I should come and live in it. He's got some fool notion of selling my life story to the movies, if you can believe that, but I say he just feels sorry for an old woman and thinks I can't do for myself."

"Anyone can see you're not an old woman," I protested.

"Well, now aren't you sweet to say it? And that's just why I told him I wasn't about to up and move to California without seeing you and that sweet Cisco one more time before Christmas." She scratched Cisco behind the ear as she spoke and then settled back with a big smile. "So how is your new kennel coming? Ready for the grand opening?"

I had told her about the delays in the construction project weeks ago, but unlike most of the residents I visited, her memory was as sharp as mine—sharper, most days. "They've got it under roof," I told her, "but we're a long way from opening. The under-floor radiant heat was a little more expensive than I expected," I confessed, "so money is running short. It might be spring before they finish up."

"You need to get yourself a rich fella," she advised with a wink. "You young people do everything the hard way these days."

I laughed a little. "I think you might be right about that, Miss Esther." The trouble was that I *had* a rich boyfriend—well, kind of—and my life was a great deal more complicated with him than without him. "When are you leaving for California?" I asked.

"Sunday, they tell me. I'm planning to be all settled in by Christmas. What about you? Are you and the pups planning a big Christmas?"

"It's always a big Christmas around my house," I told her, even though that wasn't exactly true this year. The Christmas party I usually gave for my dog-training students wouldn't be happening this year, since I had no dog-training students. Christmas dinner with Aunt Mart and Uncle Roe was bound to be awkward without Buck. And this year there would be one less stocking hung on my fireplace, since Majesty had gone to live with Aunt Mart. It's always sad to see the family getting smaller, especially at Christmastime. But then I thought about most of the residents of the nursing home, and I felt guilty for even almost feeling sorry for myself.

"And how about those cute little Australian shepherds of yours?" Esther said. "What are they doing with themselves these days?"

"Mischief has learned a new trick. She can hop up on the counter, open the cabinet, and take down her own food dish. "

"Gracious! How in the world did you teach her that?"

"Are you kidding? That's the last thing I'd want to teach her! She figured that out for herself."

We laughed and talked about dogs for a while, which was my favorite subject, and fortunately, also one of Esther's. I knew that she, like most of the people here, missed the pets of her youth, which was one reason my visits with Cisco were so valuable. But what made visiting with Esther so enjoyable for me was that she not only held up her side of the conversation, she usually had far more interesting things to say than I did.

That's why I was a little disappointed when, after chatting for only three or four minutes, she declared decisively, "Well, you've got things to do and I won't keep you." She fumbled for her cane and I put it within reach. She pulled herself to her feet. "Come on back to my room, sweetheart, I've got a little something for you."

I thought she had probably gotten someone to bring in a Christmas present for Cisco, or perhaps she had knitted me a scarf, and I was touched. "Now, Miss

Esther, I hope you didn't go to any trouble on our account."

She moved fairly well on her cane, but I had to bring Cisco into a close heel and slow our pace by half in order to stay well behind her. We edged past medicine carts and wheelchairs, I.V. stands, and half empty lunch trays, and as much confidence as I had in Cisco's training, I never took my eyes off him— particularly around the lunch trays.

We maneuvered safely through the obstacle course and reached Esther's room without incident. As soon as we were inside, she turned to me with her finger laid across her lips in a shushing gesture, poked her head outside the door, looked up and down the corridor, then quickly pulled the door closed behind us.

"A secret?" I teased her, smiling. "Well, I guess it's that time of year, isn't it?"

But Esther was not smiling when she turned away from the door. She gripped my arm with more force than I would have thought possible from such a small woman, and, leaning in close, said seriously, "Didn't I hear you were married to the sheriff?"

Terrific. It's not that I don't love explaining to people how I could have divorced a wonderful man like Buck, but this was twice in the space of an hour that the subject had come up. My Christmas spirit was starting to sink.

"Actually," I said, "I used to be, but I'm not any more. That is, he's not really the sheriff, he's just serving out my uncle's unexpired term, who *used* to be sheriff. But we're not married now." Even I was confused by that, and when I saw her eyes start to cloud over I clarified, "Acting Sheriff Lawson is my ex-husband."

She frowned a little, then said decisively, "Well, that's almost the same thing. Just as long as you have somebody to go to if things get rough. Come away from the door. I have to tell you something and I don't want anyone else to overhear. This is just between you and me."

The room was small and starkly furnished with hospital bed, a clothes locker, one guest chair and a chest of drawers. Leaning on the cane, she went over to the locker. Cisco and I followed slowly, pausing in the center of the room.

"I don't know how they found me here, but I should've known they wouldn't let me leave the state without making one more try for it." Her voice had a grim note that wasn't at all like her.

"Who?" I was starting to get a very bad feeling this had nothing to do with a gift-wrapped dog toy or a hand-knit scarf. "Who's making one more try for what?"

She swung open the door of the clothes locker and then paused, resting a moment with both hands on the handle of the cane. "Honey, will you come over here and give me hand?"

"Cisco, down." In a room that small, a dog Cisco's size seemed twice as big, so it was safer for everyone to leave him stretched out in a corner. He watched alertly as I went over to Esther. After all, he had received dog biscuits everywhere he had gone today; he had every right to expect that more were forthcoming.

There were only a few items of clothing hanging in the locker: a quilted satin robe, a couple of flannel nightgowns, and two or three velour track suits like the one she wore today. On the floor there were several pairs of shoes lined up, and overhead there was a collection of shoe boxes. "You're going to have to reach way to the back," she said. "It's the one on the bottom…That's it," she said as I stood on my tiptoes to push aside the front boxes, dragging one forward with my fingertips. "Bring that one down here."

The shoebox was so old the cardboard was soft around the corners, and part of the name of manufacturer had been worn away. But it was heavy: heavier than a scarf, and heavier than dog biscuits. I have to admit, my curiosity was aroused as I handed it over to her.

Esther tucked the box under one arm, carefully steadying herself as she released the cane, and I automatically put out my hand to hold her elbow. She removed the lid of the box and smiled as she surveyed the contents. Inside was a pair of worn and dusty leopard-print pumps.

"I danced with Jack Kennedy in these," she said, touching them fondly.

"No kidding?" I could see why she would want to hold on to them, and even go to the trouble to make certain they traveled with her to the nursing home.

"Of course," she added, "that was back during my CIA days."

I stared at her.

With one last reminiscent smile she replaced the lid on the box and, drawing in her breath significantly, she offered it to me. "Now, I don't mean to be giving you trouble," she said. "This is yours to do with as you please. You just don't let those government fellows bully you, understand? I've been keeping these safe for fifty years, and I reckon the time has come to turn the job over to somebody else. Besides…" She smiled contentedly. "My grandson says we're all going to be rich when we sell my story to the movies."

With every word she spoke my dismay deepened, and by the time she shoved the box into my hands I was just about as confused as I had ever been. She had always been so sharp and so sensible, but as fascinating as Esther's life in Hollywood had been, I seriously doubted that the CIA had been after a pair of her leopard-print pumps for half a century. And I really, really hoped she wasn't seriously counting on selling her story to the movies in order to finance her trip to California.

I said gently, "Miss Esther, are you sure you want to give these away? You danced with a president in them."

She looked at me blankly. "President of what?"

"The United States?" I prompted. "Jack Kennedy?"

"Pshaw." She gave an impatient twist of her wrist. "He wasn't President. He was just cattin' around with Marilyn."

I ventured carefully, "Monroe?"

One of the CNAs, looking perky in a red-felt Santa hat, poked her head in the door. "How's everything going in here, Miss Esther? Are you enjoying your visit with the sweet doggie?"

Esther rolled her eyes and gave me a knowing look, and for a moment she seemed more like her old self. I relaxed cautiously.

The nurse looked at me. "Raine, if you get time will you stop by Mrs. Gunfelder's room? She's been looking forward to your visit all week but she didn't feel up to coming down to the cafeteria this afternoon."

I murmured, "Of course."

But as soon as the door closed behind the nurse, Esther turned and clamped a hand on my arm again. "Now you remember what I said. You don't let them bully you, understand? The law is on your side. You get on out of here," she said, urging me to the door. "Go on, hurry, and don't let that box out of your hands until you get home, you hear me?"

I tried to extricate myself gently but she was a woman on a mission and her grip was like iron. Finally I said helplessly, "Um, my dog?"

She blinked a little and released my arm. I called Cisco to heel.

I picked up Cisco's leash and, just before we left, I turned and gave Esther a one-armed hug. "You take care of yourself, okay?   Have a wonderful trip to California. I'm going to miss you."

She patted my back affectionately, then pulled away from the hug. Her eyes were dead serious as she looked into mine. "You're a good girl, Raine Stockton, and you and Cisco have meant the world to me these last few months. You go on out and have a good life, and you let me know if you ever need anything, you hear? I've got friends with connections."

Esther Kelp might be slipping into the pleasant mental fog of old age, complete with its delusions and oddities, but there was no denying the sincerity of her intentions.   "Thank you, Miss Esther," I told her, smiling. I held up the box. "And thank you for these. I know what they must have meant to you. I'll treasure them."

But with all that happened later, it was several days before I remembered to bring it in from the car, and then I stuck it in the room with the Christmas decorations and all but forgot about it.

I suppose what happened later served me right.

FOUR

I live in the same white-columned farmhouse that my ancestors built in 1869, which is nestled at the base of Hawk Mountain on the edge of a national forest. Deer graze on my apple tree and use my driveway as a shortcut to their beds. Foxes and raccoons give the dogs plenty to stay excited about, and every now and then a bear will wander down from the hills and make himself known on my front porch. Bobcats and coyote leave pawprints in the snow on my lawn. I can't imagine living anywhere else.

Dog Daze Boarding and Training is located behind the house, where the original barn had been. After a small fire had caused enough smoke and water damage to justify a major remodel, I had decided to expand and upgrade with an indoor training room large enough to set up a small agility course, in-floor heating, and twenty individual indoor-outdoor kennel runs. As with most construction projects, it had quickly gotten out of hand. I had been promised a fully-functional, bright and gleaming kennel facility complete with happy, barking dogs before Christmas. What I had was an empty shell of a building with no heat, no electricity, no plumbing, and, needless to say, no dogs. Just looking at the deserted structure every time I drove up depressed me.

It was not even five o'clock when I got home, but the sun had already set behind my mountain and the twilight was deep. My headlights flashed first on the red metal roof of Dog Daze as I came over the slight rise of the long gravel drive that led from the road, and then on the dark windows of my house. I had just enough time to feed the dogs, change into my shepherdess costume, and hopefully grab a bite to eat in town before I had to take my place in the Christmas parade lineup with Mystery and the sheep. I parked in front of the house, opened the back of the SUV for Cisco, and the two of us hurried up the steps.

The first thing I noticed when I flipped on the lights was a silver Christmas ornament in the middle of the floor. I bent to pick it up and noticed another, a few feet away, and another beyond that. I was starting to get a bad feeling, and I muttered under my breath, "Mischief." I had taken a box of Christmas ornaments down from the attic yesterday, but had made certain to put it on top of the highboy in the dining room before I left this afternoon. Mischief and Magic were of course crated whenever I was away, but a locked door to Mischief was more of a suggestion than an impediment, so I always double-checked to make certain all valuables, breakables, and dangerous items were well out of reach before I left her alone. But sometimes even double- and triple-checking was not enough.

While Cisco bounded ahead to explore on his own, I followed the trail of shiny Christmas balls down the hallway and into the dining room, where I found the big cardboard box of Christmas decorations that had been safely stored on top of the five-foot-tall highboy now sitting in the middle of the floor. It wasn't overturned; it wasn't shredded. It was just sitting there, its contents neatly unpacked around it—three tidily wound strands of lights, four boxes of tiny glitter stars stacked one on top of the other, and two boxes of silver Christmas balls, one of which was empty.

I dumped the silver ornaments that I had collected into the box and hurried to the living room, calling, "Mischief! Where are you? Mischief!"

I stopped short in front of the two crates, sitting side by side, each complete with a grinning Australian shepherd inside. My heart skipped a beat. Once before I had come home to a house in disarray and had blamed the dogs when it had, in fact, been an intruder. I cast a quick, alarmed look over my shoulder before reminding myself that if anyone had been in my house who did not belong there, Cisco would have alerted me by now—and a burglar probably would have done something more inventive than unpack Christmas ornaments. That was when something shiny in Magic's crate caught my eye. A silver Christmas ball.

I bent down to examine both crates more closely. The doors were closed, but the slide bolts on each door were not engaged. I had known Mischief to unlock her own crate before, and had even gone through a phase of tying the crate door closed—until Mischief learned to chew through the ties. I stepped back from the crates, stood up straight, and said, "Okay, girls, release."

Mischief hooked one paw through the grate of the crate door, swung it open, and walked out, her tailless butt wriggling madly as she came to greet me. I couldn't help laughing, with both astonishment and exasperation, as Magic carefully picked up the silver ball between her teeth, pushed open the door with her nose, and bounded over to me.

"You girls are too smart for you own good, do you know that?" I took the shiny ball out of Magic's mouth; it was plastic coated and less likely to break than the glass ones, but still it wasn't the kind of thing you want your dog playing with. I tried to look stern as I turned to Mischief, but ruined the effect by rubbing her fur affectionately from head to tail. "So what's the story? You sneak out of your crate, spend the day playing with Christmas ornaments, then sneak back in when you hear my car pull up? And now you're sharing the fun with your sister?"

Mischief grinned up at me in absolute agreement, then favored me with an excited blur-spin and raced off to the kitchen. Magic scurried after her, and because this day's work had only served to remind me what could happen when they were left unsupervised, I didn't waste any time before I followed them.

I scooped dog food into the bowls of three worshipfully fixated dogs, set their dishes on the floor, and released them to eat. I then hurried upstairs to grab my costume, dialing Sonny as I went. "How did it go?" I asked when she answered on the third ring.

Parade coordinators had volunteered themselves and their animal trailers to transport the livestock and the three sheep Sonny had chosen as the most docile at 3:00 that afternoon. She chortled with pride as she described how Mystery had marched the sheep into the trailer like the Pied Piper. "Mr. Samuels tried to buy her from me on the spot," she said, "and he doesn't even have sheep! He was still shaking his head over it when he drove off. Of course, Mystery is a little upset. She doesn't understand why the sheep left without her."

"Just tell her that she's going to get her chance to show them off in a couple of hours." I wriggled out of the jingle-bell sweater and into a heavy-duty sweatshirt that would keep me warm under the costume as I spoke, juggling the telephone from one ear to the other.

"I did," Sonny assured me. "But her concept of time is a little different than ours."

I should mention that Sonny, who is in all other respects a perfectly rational woman and a highly respected attorney-at-law, occasionally has "intuitive glimpses" into the thoughts of animals. In other words, she talks to dogs. And worse, sometimes they answer her.

I said, "I'm going to head out in a few minutes. Do you want to meet at Miss Meg's for a quick sandwich before the parade?" I pulled off my stylish wedge-heeled boots and sat down on the bed to pull on a pair of heavy wool socks.

"I'd better not. You know how Mystery is about being left in the car. I thought we'd plan to get there right before the sheep are unloaded."

"Probably a good idea." If Mystery saw her sheep locked up where she could not get to them, she would have a barking fit that would send every animal in the line-up into stampede mode.

"Mr. Samuels said they're going to start moving out of the City Hall parking lot at 6:00, so I figure if we get there by 6:10, it should be just right." For obvious reasons, the live animals were always last in the parade. "I'll park where I can see you."

"Okay, I'll give you a wave when we're ready for Mystery." Cradling the phone between my shoulder and ear, I pulled on one of my rubber-soled boots. I had walked in these parades before. "What do you think the chances are of this thing going off without a hitch?"

"Let's see. Llamas, horses, sheep, a donkey and an entire contingent of dogs from the humane society with twinkling lights around their necks." That part, I knew, was my Aunt Mart's idea. Since my Majesty had gone to live with her she lost no chance to volunteer for any charity that would welcome collies, and Majesty would be leading the humane society group tonight—with twinkling lights around her neck. "Not to mention fire engines, cheerleaders, Shriners, twenty floats with multiple moving parts, and a forty-foot-tall Christmas tree. I'd say about one in two hundred."

"That high?" I pulled on my last boot and stood. "It'll never hold up in Vegas. Okay, I'm on my way. See you there."

I grabbed my costume—a floor length burlap muumuu and a shepherd's crook—and raced down stairs just as the dogs were finishing their dinner. I let them out into the fenced exercise yard while I touched up my makeup—not that shepherdesses, traditionally, worried much about that sort of thing. I put the Aussies back in their crates and settled Cisco with a bone, and was back in my car before the engine even cooled off.

And that was pretty much the way my life would be from now until Christmas.

During most of the year Hanover County is home to about four thousand people. In the summer that number can easily double, and during the Christmas season, there are enough people from Raleigh and Charleston and Atlanta who decide to spend the season in their mountain vacation homes that the small town of Hansonville can feel even smaller very quickly. We are thirty minutes from the Far Heights Ski Resort, which has man-made snow from November through March, and only two hours from Asheville, in case the tourists get a yen for the big city. Between Thanksgiving and New Year's, the rent on lake cabins doubles. Sometimes the holidays in Hansonville can feel like summer without the sunshine.

When I drove into town there wasn't a parking place left and the sidewalks were already starting to fill with eager parade-viewers. Someone was selling hot chocolate and children in knit hats were warming their hands around paper cups of it. All the storefronts had their twinkling lights on, and in combination with the wrapped lamp posts, the illuminated sleigh and reindeer atop the department store, and the strands of multicolored lights that looped between the two traffic lights on Main Street, the entire town looked like a fairy land. I didn't blame the part-timers for wanting to spend Christmas here.

I drove around the barricade at City Hall and parked in one of the spots reserved for volunteers, waving to a couple of people I knew as I got out. The parking lot was already a melee of winter-wonderland floats on flatbed trucks, little elves in green felt and red tutus, and pickup trucks decorated with evergreen and miles of lights. The animal staging area was actually along a side street that ran behind City Hall, well away from the noise and chaos of main parking lot—which was just as well, because the animal area had enough noise and chaos of its own.

The members of the riding club, who always proudly led the rear of the parade, were busy securing battery-operated red lights to their horses' saddles and hooves. The donkey was braying. The llamas poked their heads over the high planks of their trailer, looking big-eyed and scared. A dozen freshly shampooed refugees from our temporary animal shelter were barking and lunging in abandoned celebration of their night of unexpected freedom, their collars dancing with flashing Christmas lights. I spotted my business partner, Maude, with her two regal Goldens, River and Rune, talking with Aunt Mart.

River and Rune held championship field trial and obedience titles, and were of course lying in perfect, sphinx-like down-stays at Maude's feet. Majesty's only title was the one she had awarded herself—Queen of the Universe—and she wore it as proudly as she wore the wreath of red velvet bows and twinkle lights around her snowy mane. She marched to the end of her leash around Aunt Mart's feet, head alert, occasionally issuing a sharp bark to something or someone she felt was on the verge of stepping out of line. She was in her element.

I barely greeted my aunt and my friend as I dropped immediately to my knees and hugged Majesty, exclaiming over how beautiful she looked. My aunt beamed at me fondly, and Majesty greeted me with a polite dart of her Collie tongue on my cheek, then went back to her patrol of the perimeter. "So how's it going?" I asked as I got to my feet.

"Bloody disaster in the making, if you ask me," replied Maude cheerfully. "You don't bring untrained dogs out in the midst of this circus, not to make mention of what the llamas and the sheep are doing to the herding breeds. And if one of those horses doesn't spook and throw its rider before the night is done they all deserve a bloody gold medal." Despite having been in this country for forty of her sixty-something years, Maude had never lost her crisp British accept, which always added a certain weight to what she said. "I tried to tell Dolly, but she was having nothing but her way, as usual."

Dolly Amstead was perhaps the most organized person on the East Coast. She was in charge of just about everything that needed doing—the animal shelter, the Christmas pageant, the food drive, and of course the Christmas parade. Customarily we used only trained and tested dogs to represent the interests of the humane society: Maude with River and Rune, me with Cisco, and whatever volunteers from nearby dog clubs we could get to walk with us. Dolly had unilaterally decided that it would be much more effective to have the dogs who were available for adoption walk in the parade this year. The secret to her success, apparently, was "damn the torpedoes, full speed ahead."

Aunt Mart said, "Well, perhaps it will all work out. Everything certainly does look festive, doesn't it?"

I grinned at her. "Majesty is the most festive looking one of all of them. I hope you brought your camera."

Aunt Mart happily reached into the pocket of her red wool coat and brought out her palm camera. I posed with Majesty and she snapped my picture.

Technically, Aunt Mart and I had a temporary shared- custody agreement regarding Majesty, but as far Majesty was concerned, she had found her Forever home. Majesty needed to be the center of attention, and Aunt Mart needed someone to dote on. And though I missed my collie terribly, the truth was that they were probably a match made in heaven.

I said, "I've got to check on the sheep, and then I'm going to run over to Miss Meg's and get a sandwich. Can I bring anyone back something?"

"Coffee would be lovely, dear, if you don't mind," Aunt Mart said. "It's already a bit brisk, isn't it?"

"It's supposed to be in the twenties again tonight," I said. "I hope they get this thing moving on time."

"The Fuhrer assures us the first marching band will march at precisely six o'clock," Maude said dryly, and I laughed and waved over my shoulder as I hurried off to check on the sheep.

Miss Meg's was crowded with parade-goers, as I should have known it would be, and there was a wait for seating that pressed against the door. I inched inside and stood on tiptoe to peer over the heads in front of me, wondering if I would be better off dashing into the drugstore for a candy bar, when I saw a familiar face toward the front of the crowd. Unfortunately, he saw me too.

"Raine," he called and waved me forward. It was the only polite thing to do.

And the only polite thing for me to do was to return the best smile I could manage and, murmuring one apology after another, edge my way through the crowd. Of course the crowd parted for me without hesitance. He was, after all, the sheriff.

"Hey, Buck," I said. "How's it going?" I was trying very hard to keep our relationship cordial, and some days I succeeded better than others. In the spirit of Christmas, I had resolved to put forth my best effort on every occasion.

"About like you'd expect this time of year." He was in uniform, his radio crackling on low volume on his shoulder. His eyes wandered around the room, looking for the hostess. I figured his dinner break would be his only chance to sit down tonight, and he probably wanted to get started on it. "Shoplifters, burglaries, pickpockets, and people stealing baby Jesuses from mangers. 'Tis the season, and all that."

I blinked. "Baby Jesus?"

"Sure." He caught Meg's eye and lifted his hand. "The Baptist church had to replace two of them last week, and the Christmas Shop is keeping them behind the counter. It's a thing with kids, like stealing garden gnomes."

Looking harried, Meg arrived with an order pad in her hand and a pair of Santa earrings dangling from her ears. "Sorry, Buck. Have you ever seen the like? Everybody wants to eat early for the parade, I guess. I've got a table cleaned off for you. Come on back. Hi, Raine. You two together?"

While she waited for an answer, I felt awkward and Buck looked embarrassed. Then Buck, who was never uncomfortable about anything for long, said, "Come on, Raine, no sense in both of us waiting for a table." And he started to follow Meg.

Well, terrific. I was starving, but a person had to draw the line somewhere. And I thought having dinner with my ex-husband—who, by the way, was practically living with another woman—at the most popular restaurant in town just like old times might be just a tad over that line. I said quickly, "Actually I already ate. I just came over to get a cup of coffee for Aunt Mart. I have to get back. I'm helping set up for the parade, you know." I hoped he couldn't hear my stomach growl.

I couldn't tell whether he was relieved, disappointed, or completely indifferent. All he said was, "Okay, see you later." And Meg called over her shoulder, "Nancy! Coffee to go!" as she led him away.

I edged my way to the counter to pick up my coffee, scanning the selection of pies and cakes and wondering whether I could get a slice to go. I saw Nancy hold up my coffee in a to-go cup, and I tried to get her attention to call out an order for pie, but there were three people in line ahead of me and she simply set the coffee beside the cashier's stand and rushed off. I was behind a big guy in camouflage who kept shuffling his feet back and forth, so it was possible she didn't see me. Disappointed, I dug a dollar bill out of my pocket to pay for the coffee and waited my turn.

I saw Ruth Holloway and her husband, Jack, a couple of tables over and waved to them. "Ready for your big night?" I called.

"Mary and Joseph at your service," she called back, toasting me with a French fry, and Jack, not to be outdone, added, "Hope they've got room for us at the inn."

Ruth elbowed him in the ribs for the bad joke, and I was about to make an equally bad one back when I was distracted by a slight disturbance in the line in front of me. The guy in camouflage had reached the cashier and I was aware that this was the second time she had given him his total. He patted his pockets, looking for his wallet, and finally dug a bill out, frowning at it for a moment, before he turned it over to her. That was when I noticed he was wearing a buck knife in a leather sheath strapped to his belt, not something you see every day, even around here. He smelled of wild dead things and a couple of days without a shower, and I figured he must have been returning from an overnight hunting trip.

"Ten twenty- five," Lucy, the cashier, repeated. A note of impatience was just starting to creep into her voice.

He muttered something to her I didn't hear.

"A quarter," she repeated. "I need a quarter."

He dug into his pants pocket again and took out a couple of lint-covered antacids, a pocketknife, some washers, a crumpled receipt, and a gold wedding ring. He spread them out on the counter. He said, almost in disbelief, "That's it."

Lucy looked over her shoulder for her supervisor, and I could feel the line behind me growing restless. I reached into my pocket one more time, scraped out a quarter, and reached around to hand it to Lucy. "Merry Christmas," I said to the hunter.

He had greasy black hair and a full dark beard, and he looked at me with a stunned, uncomprehending expression. Abruptly, he muttered something I did not hear, swept the items on the counter back into his pocket, and shouldered past me and out the door.

I made a face of exaggerated question to Lucy, and she shrugged. "Weirdo," she said, ringing up my order. "Did you see the blood on his jacket? Jeez, I wish these guys would clean up a little before they come in here. That'll be a dollar three for the coffee."

I managed to scrape another nickel out of my pocket. "Keep the change. Who was that guy anyway?"

She shrugged and dropped my two cents change into the Need a Penny,Take a Penny jar. "We get all kinds on Parade night."

"Well, have a good Christmas. I hope you get a chance to see the parade."

I turned to go and stepped on something hard. "Oh-oh." I picked it up and held it out between thumb and forefinger to Lucy. "That guy dropped his wedding ring." I held it up to the light and saw there was writing inside. *Forever, Amy.* "His wife is going to kill him."

"I'll keep it in the cash register." Lucy took the ring and waved the next customer forward. "I hope he remembers where he lost it."

But apparently he didn't, or maybe he didn't think it was worth coming back for. Lucy tucked the ring under the cash tray and forgot about it, and neither one of us ever saw Camo Man again.

FIVE

Dolly Amstead, parade master extraordinaire, made certain that the first drum sounded and the first baton twirled at precisely 6:00. Sonny arrived with Mystery at 6:10 and the sheep were marching down the ramp like little soldiers at 6:15. It really was something to see.

Maude and I had gone to battle with Dolly to leave fifteen feet between the last float, Reardon Real Estate's "Home is Where the Heart Is" (which would probably win the Most Artistic award for its charming re-creation of an old- fashioned parlor with grandma snoozing in the rocker and Santa's legs dangling from the fireplace), and the first animal walkers. She had compromised by putting the riding club between the real estate float with "I'll Be Home for Christmas" blaring from its speakers and the humane society dogs. The riding club did look sharp in their white Stetsons, white vests, and white boots—all artistically decorated in red twinkling lights—astride their only slightly nervous steeds all decked out in white saddle blankets and saddles trimmed in matching red lights, with red lights twinkling on their hooves. By this time I was starting to wish I'd had the battery-operated twinkle lights concession for this parade, because they were certainly the most popular item of the evening.

Maude, who would never undermine the dignity of her dogs with costuming, was next, walking with River and Rune, who held a banner between them that read "Adopt a Pet". They got roars from the crowd as they marched by, each dog holding a corner of the sign in his mouth. Following them, Aunt Mart walked proudly with Majesty, who wore a saddlebag sign that read "Spay or Neuter" on either side. I have to admit, the twinkling lights that were draped through Majesty's flowing white collar did give her a certain flare. Behind them, barking and lunging and pulling their handlers from side to side, came the humane society dogs. I breathed a silent prayer of thanks that I hadn't volunteered to be in charge of *that* part of the parade. If all of those dogs made it back to the transport van without escaping their handlers or knocking down someone's toddler, it would be a miracle.

I was happy to let Mary and Joseph with the donkey go next, followed by the three wise men with their llamas. The sheep huddled together close to the trailer baaing and shuffling nervously, and Mystery was in her border-collie crouch, her eyes fixed on her herd, waiting for one of them to step out of line. Dolly stood on the back of one of the empty trailers with her director's clipboard and her stop watch, half-glasses perched on her nose, her hand raised in readiness as she counted down the number of steps the llamas took. She began to fold down her fingers: *Five four, three…*

"Okay, Mystery," I said, swallowing hard and trying not to be nervous. "I'm counting on you, girl. Show 'em your stuff."

This might be a good time to mention that Mystery had never had a herding lesson. Neither had I. It had sounded like such a good idea when we came up with it, since there was absolutely nothing that could give me more joy than showing off a beautiful working dog, and of course Sonny had all the confidence in the world in her pet. Dolly was an easy sell, because she believed with absolute certainty that there wasn't a sheep in the world—or a dog—who would dare to spoil her perfectly choreographed parade by stepping out of line. I certainly hoped she was right, because it was beginning to occur to me for the first time that herding sheep in her own back yard and marching sheep down Main Street in the midst of a noisy parade with cheering crowds on either side were two very different things, even for a dog as gifted as Mystery.

Two, one…

"Mystery," I said, "you're on!"

For one truly endless moment, nothing happened. The sheep baaed; Mystery crouched. Then, in an act of desperation rather than inspiration, I poked the lead sheep in the butt with my crook. He gave an indignant bleat and lurched forward, and we were off.

It may be true that fortune favors the foolish, or maybe we had a guardian angel or two, because among six wild dogs, ten horses, two llamas, a donkey, three sheep and a border collie, there was not a single incident. No one bit or was bitten, no one was thrown or stampeded or trampled. And, looking back, perhaps the most amazing thing of all was that Mystery, who had never had a single herding lesson, managed to keep her three sheep in a straight line for six blocks, despite cheering crowds, barking dogs, flashing lights, and children throwing popcorn. At the time, of course, I wasn't thinking about fortunes or angels. I was concentrating on watching every step the sheep took, counting each block, and promising myself I'd never volunteer for anything ever again.

Most people think of sheep as docile creatures, but I had seen them kick like mules and leap over the heads of full grown men. Logically I knew that Sonny's sheep were more like pets than barn animals, that they were completely submissive to Mystery, and that if Sonny had not had complete faith in the plan she never would have signed up for it. But in my experience with events like this anything that could go wrong, would go wrong. That was why, when we reached the parade route end at town square where the Nativity was set up and the giant tree was ready to be lit, I simply couldn't believe it; everything had gone off without a hitch.

The plan was for Sonny to meet me at the town square and take over the role as shepherdess for the rest of the evening, and she was waiting as we had agreed. I gave her a big grin and a thumbs-up, still hardly believing we had pulled it off. There was a pen for the sheep toward the back of the crèche, and Sonny opened the gate as we approached, calling to Mystery. I heard a round of applause go up as Mystery herded the sheep into the pen and Sonny closed the gate. My grin broadened.

While Joseph helped Mary off the donkey and tethered the beast to a stake in the ground provided for that purpose, I quickly stepped out of the burlap caftan and helped Sonny into it. The transformation was complete before the wise men even got their llamas in place.

"Unbelievable," I said, as the children's choir began to sing "Silent Night". "Who would have thought we could pull this off?"

"Why, my dear," returned Sonny, "I never doubted Dolly for a moment." And she added dryly, "No one was allowed to."

I tried not to giggle. "Mystery is a rock star. She doesn't need to take herding lessons. She needs to give them."

"She knows." Sonny smiled indulgently at her dog, who was lying at attention outside the sheep pen. "The problem is going to be trying to get her back in the car."

"Not a single hitch," I reiterated wonderingly. "Who would have believed it?"

We stood in a kind of awed self-congratulations as the choir finished "Silent Night" and then, right on cue, the great tree sprang to life with a thousand brilliant, multicolored lights. A cheer of delight went up from the crowd, and the choir broke into "Oh, Christmas Tree". The air was cold and crisp, the sheep were bleating the background, children were singing in the foreground, and somewhere a dog barked. I stood bathed in the glow of the sparkling Christmas lights and thought that there had never been a more perfect Christmas moment.

And then Dolly arrived.

She was a stylish woman in black leggings and a short wool coat with a faux-fur collar. Her ankle boots had a stacked heel and she wore festive red-framed half-glasses and dangling Christmas-wreath earrings. She carried her clipboard and counted heads with her pen. "Okay, Wise Men, front and center. You're supposed to be kneeling around the manger. Where's your frankincense and myrrh?"

"I told you, Dolly, I have a bad knee," Rob Adams complained. "Can't I worship standing up?"

"Somebody should stay with the llamas," added Burt Tompkins, who owned them. "They're sensitive animals."

Dolly opened her mouth to reply, and Sonny distracted her with, "Everything went beautifully, Dolly. Congratulations."

"Well, of course it did," replied Dolly, and she frowned a little. "Can't you quiet down those sheep?"

The sheep were getting vocal, and one in particular was giving off a persistent bleat that could be heard above the singing. I glanced at the pen but couldn't see anything that was disturbing them.

Dolly stared at me. "What are you still doing here? Weren't you scheduled to walk only?"

I held up both hands in a peace-loving gesture. "On my way. I was just making sure the sheep were secure."

"Well, hurry up. You're spoiling the vignette. Mary, Joseph, at the manger, please. Mary, you're sitting, and, Joseph, stand at her right side."

"Should I be holding the baby or not?" Ruth Holloway inquired.

"Holding, holding," Dolly said impatiently. "While on duty, the babe is in arms. When you leave at night, return him to the manger."

Since no one had volunteered a real infant for the living Nativity, Dolly had been forced to compromise with a doll. It was supposed to be one of those life-like ones with pudgy little hands and dimples that made you look twice, but it was still a doll. I thought Dolly was a little put out by that.

"Better be careful about leaving it here at night," I advised. "Buck said there's been a rash of baby Jesus thefts."

Everyone stared at me. "What?" For the first time that evening, Dolly actually seemed to miss a beat. "Did you say 'baby Jesus thefts'?"

"No lie."

And one of the wise men shook his head sadly. "What is this world coming to?"

The choir started singing "Here Comes Santa Claus". The sheep bleated louder. Ruth bent forward to pick up the baby Jesus and then stopped, frozen. "Oh, my God."

I think we all realized at the same time that the bleating we heard was not coming from the sheep pen, after all, but the manger. Everyone realized it, that is, except Kitty, who exclaimed indignantly, "Don't tell me someone has stolen our baby Jesus. Don't you dare tell me that!"

"Okay," Ruth said softly. She bent forward and gently, wonderingly, lifted a bundle of living, bleating, fist-flailing infant from the manger. "I won't."

Dolly stared at the baby. We all stared at the baby. "That," Dolly said flatly, "was not supposed to happen."

Did I call it? There was no way this thing was going to go off without a hitch.

We all surged forward at once. The baby was wrapped in a pilled blue fleece blanket that looked as though it had come from an adult-sized bed, which is most likely what had kept the infant from freezing. Still, its little fists were shaking and its screams were growing hoarser. Ruth carefully peeled back some of the folds of the blanket to reveal a very tiny, completely naked, baby girl.

Dolly looked around the crowd imperiously and demanded, "Whose infant is this?"

"Oh, for heaven's sake, Dolly, it's clearly an abandoned newborn," Sonny said.

"Probably only a few hours old." Ruth rewrapped the baby in the blanket and held it close, trying to soothe it with a bouncing motion. "The umbilical stump isn't even dry."

"Oh, good heavens," declared Dolly with an expression of the utmost displeasure. She snatched a walkie-talkie from her pocket and spoke into it. "We need a paramedic at the living Nativity. We have an unauthorized infant on the premises."

Later, when I was telling the story to Maude and Aunt Mart, they made me repeat that part twice.

It is a testament to Dolly's iron will and undisputed talent for controlling the uncontrollable that, even with most of the town gathered around, there was very little disruption in the ceremonies, and many people didn't even know what had happened until they read about it in the weekly paper. Our one rescue unit was of course on-site, and it took the EMT about three minutes to walk to the scene with his emergency bag. By this time Dolly had shooed Ruth, who refused to relinquish the baby to anyone except the paramedic, outside the crèche and behind it. Of course her husband insisted upon going with her, which left our Nativity minus two rather important characters. But when everyone else in the scene started to trail after them curiously, Dolly was having none of it. She controlled her players like Mystery controlled her sheep – when the evil eye wasn't strong enough, a sharp bark or a little nip always did the trick.

I scooted out of the way before I was drafted into playing Mary and hurried around to the back of our plywood stable where Mike Keller, the paramedic, was listening to the baby's heartbeat with a stethoscope while Ruth held her. I waited until he removed the earpieces before I said, "What do you think, Mike?"

He took out a penlight and shone it in the baby's eyes. The poor thing screamed harder. "She's seems okay so far, all things considered." He tore open a small plastic package and snapped out a silver space blanket. "This'll warm her up a lot faster," he told Ruth. He tucked the space blanket inside the folds of the big bed blanket and began to swaddle the baby. "We'll take her to the hospital and have them check her out. Not more than a day old, I'd say." And he gave a short shake of his head, his tone tight, "She could have frozen to death. All the mother had to do was drop her off at any hospital or fire station, no questions asked. We need a public awareness campaign on that."

I glanced at Ruth and knew we were both thinking the same thing. "I don't know, Mike," I said. "In a town this small, 'no questions asked' doesn't mean much."

The children were singing "Frosty the Snowman". A few people passed by and looked at us curiously.

Ruth relinquished the infant to Mike reluctantly, her expression uneasy. "What will happen to her? Do you really think she'll be okay?"

Mike said, "The hospital will take good care of her, don't you worry. After that, social services. The police will want to talk to everyone who was there when she was found, so y'all hang tight. A deputy will be up here shortly."

"He's got his work cut out for him," I said. "There must've been five hundred people in the square when she was found, not to mention everybody who was in and out all day."

"Well, the manger didn't go up until four o'clock," Jack Holloway pointed out. "I know, because I helped set it up."

"That's good," Mike said. "At least we know she couldn't have been out here more than a couple of hours." The baby started to whimper again, and Ruth reached out a solicitous hand. "Let me get this little one in the ambulance where it's warm," Mike said. "You can call the hospital if you want to check on her."

Jack put his arm around Ruth's shoulders as Mike slung the strap of his bag over his shoulder and hurried away. I remembered what Ruth had told me in the classroom that afternoon about wanting to have a baby and hoping that their roles in the Nativity would bring them luck, and I could see a mixture of wonder, yearning and hope on her face as she watched them go. I couldn't help but feel a little shiver of superstitious wonder myself.

Ruth said anxiously, "She's so tiny." She looked up at her husband. "Do you think we should go to the hospital with her? It doesn't seem right that she should just be carted off like luggage or something. She should have someone to take care of her on the ride."

"Mike is terrific with kids," I assured her. "He's got three of his own."

Jack added gently, "We'll call the hospital later, okay? Let's go tell everyone she's okay."

Ruth frowned a little. "You don't suppose Dolly is really going to go through with the living Nativity tonight, do you?"

"If I know Dolly, and I do, she will," I assured her. "And the less fuss we make about it the better for everyone concerned."

Jack gave a wry half smile. "She's right, hon. There are going to be a bunch of kids lined up wanting to pet the donkeys and the sheep as soon as the choir finishes, and we're part of the act. Let's get back."

I said, "Hey, Jack. When you set up the manger, was there a doll in it?"

He thought for a moment. "Yeah, come to think of it, Dolly came by just as we were leaving and left the doll. It was wrapped in a scarf or something the same color as Ruth's robe. They were supposed to match."

I nodded. "I wonder what happened to it."

Jack looked at me curiously and I explained, "Whoever took the doll out of the manger to put the real baby in had to get rid of the doll somewhere." I shrugged. "You guys had better get back before Dolly comes after you. I'll have a look around."

Of course it wasn't my job to look around, but I was curious. If I were a desperate young mother looking to anonymously exchange a real baby for a doll in the middle of town square with all kinds of people milling about, I probably wouldn't have wanted to carry the stolen doll very far. I poked around the stable as best I could, looking behind bales of hay and underneath the straw that lined the manger, in the shadows behind the stable and in the corners inside. I wished I had brought Cisco with me. He had an uncanny knack for sticking his nose in places it didn't belong, and he loved toys—especially when they didn't belong to him. If the doll had been hidden anywhere around here, he would have found it. I borrowed the shepherd's crook to stir around the contents of the two nearest trash barrels, but I didn't find anything bigger than a half-eaten corndog. By that time Deke, Buck's number one deputy, had arrived, and I was reminded that I was starving.

"Where's Buck?" I asked him. Buck usually liked to handle this kind of thing himself.

"Got a call," Deke replied truculently, and scowled at the notepad he took out of his pocket. Since our divorce had become final, some of the men on the force felt it was a sign of their loyalty to Buck to be rude to me whenever possible. "You know anything about this?"

"No," I admitted.

"Get on out of here, then."

I returned his scowl, but I really didn't want to get into an argument with him that would delay my dinner even further, so I turned away, muttering, "Great police work, sport." But my natural sense of good citizenship got the better of me, so I turned back and added, "The doll is missing."

He glared at me. "What doll?"

I pointed at Jack, who had taken his place with Mary in front of the empty manger. "Ask Joseph," I suggested and waved goodbye as I made my way through the crowd.

I stopped to bring Maude and Aunt Mart up to speed on events, so that by the time I walked into Miss Meg's Diner there were only a few customers left — mostly old men who had seen enough Christmas parades in their lifetime and were enjoying a cup of coffee and ESPN turned on low at the counter. I ordered a barbecue sandwich with extra French fries and sweet tea before I even sat down, then sank into a booth by the window, stretching out my legs.

I rarely came into town without one of the dogs, so it was a treat to be able to lean back, relax and enjoy a meal in a restaurant without worrying about who was waiting for me in the car. The view of the Christmas tree was spectacular from my seat in the window, and as far as I could tell the police investigation hadn't disrupted the festivities much at all. I had finished my sandwich and was swirling the last few fries around in a paper cup of ketchup, contemplating the last slice of lemon meringue pie that was displayed inside the cooler by the counter, when the bell over the door jingled and Miles Young walked in.

Miles is, for all intents and purposes, the man behind Hansonville's spectacular Christmas parade this year. Because of him, Reardon Real Estate could afford a prize-winning float with lights *and* sound. Because of him, our new animal shelter was well underway and the stray dogs had twinkle lights on their collars. Because of his tax money, the Christmas tree had new lights and the volunteer fire department had a new engine. I had heard he had also given generously to churches, food drives and under-privileged children's groups. He was Mr. Popularity around these parts lately, but I remained skeptical.

Miles Young knew how to run a PR campaign, and that was exactly what he was doing; it was no coincidence that every time he wrote a check he was smiling into the camera. He had done enough interviews about what a positive impact his new resort development was going to have on our county to run for office. Because of him, my beautiful mountain was scarred with deadfalls and roadbeds, wildlife was being displaced, and someday soon a multi-million dollar country club would be looking down on my back yard. But because of him, construction workers— the industry that had been hardest hit by the recession in our area—had jobs and children had presents under the tree. It was hard for most people to hate him these days. Myself included.

He stopped at the counter and placed an order. Then he saw me and came over, accompanied some distance behind by a young girl in a green puff coat and red toboggan hat who appeared to be attached to an electronic tablet by a set of earphones. Her eyes never left the screen as she trudged across the room.

Miles grinned as he reached me and leaned down to kiss my cheek, bringing with him the smell of the cold outdoors and Polo cologne. "Great job with those sheep, sugar. I was rooting for you."

I wriggled uncomfortably, glancing around to see who had noticed. "Miles, please. No PDAs." But my stomach fluttered with pleasure and my heartbeat had a ridiculous little catch in it. There's no accounting for chemistry. Absolutely none.

I probably should have mentioned Miles Young is the "kind of" rich boyfriend Miss Esther thought I should have. It's not that he's kind of rich; he's very rich. It's that he's kind of my boyfriend. The kind-of part refers to the fact that I think he thinks he wants to be my boyfriend; I am very far from being sure. At all.

I added, "I didn't know you were in town."

"We just got in in time for the parade." He slid into the seat opposite me and stretched out his hand for the girl, beckoning her over. She plopped down beside him without looking up.

I raised an eyebrow. "And who's this?"

Miles reached over and plucked off her hat, tugging one of the ear buds out of her ear. "Mel," he said to the little girl, "say hello to Miss Stockton. Raine, this is Melanie. My daughter."

SIX

I'll admit it, I was surprised. I'm not sure why, but I'd never thought of Miles as having children. There was no reason he shouldn't have children. I knew he was divorced, and he was in his forties, after all. But I was surprised.

I had never dated a man with children before.

I tried to hide my reaction with a quick smile to the girl. "Nice to meet you, Melanie," I said.

She muttered something without looking up.

She was probably nine or ten, a little on the plump side, with a riot of brown curly hair that was currently suffering from an unfortunate chin-length cut that caused it to stick out in all directions. She wore black-framed cat-woman glasses that were so unattractive I knew her mother had let her pick them out for herself. This, I knew, was the acclaimed "awkward phase" all girls went through just before puberty. I remembered it all too well.

I glanced at Miles, still smiling. "I didn't know you had a daughter."

Before he could answer she said, still without looking up, "Bet you didn't know he had three ex-wives, either."

My smile was starting to feel a little frozen. "No. I didn't."

Meg arrived with a cup of coffee for Miles and a mug of hot chocolate for Melanie. She set the last slice of lemon pie before Miles.

My smile faded. "I was going to order that."

Miles said to Meg, "Bring another fork, will you, Meg?"

"Sure thing, Mr. Young."

Okay, I've said it before; I'm not that wild about kids. It's not that I don't like them, exactly; it's just that I don't see the point in them. They're messy and noisy and not that interesting. They're always asking questions. They make every conversation a chore and I'd rather have dinner with a three-year-old golden retriever than a three-year-old child any day. In fact, I'm always a little suspicious of hotels that allow children but ban pets, and I avoid them when I can.

But because part of having a therapy dog often involves working with children, I have learned how to be polite to them. So I turned to Melanie and inquired pleasantly, "How old are you, Melanie?"

She did not look up. "How old are you?"

I stared at her. I made a few sputtering noises that were punctuated by a nervous laugh. I looked at Miles, expecting him to correct his daughter, but he was busy smiling his thanks at Meg as he accepted the second fork. My mother would have marched me right out of the restaurant and made me wait in the car if I had ever even thought of being so rude to an adult, but all Miles said to his little girl was, "Are you sure you don't want some of this pie, honey?"

"I told you, I hate lemon. Can I get back to my movie now?" And, not waiting for an answer, she stuffed the other ear bud back into her ear and tuned us out.

Frankly, I was glad.

Miles pushed the pie to the center of the table and I accepted the fork he offered, stabbing off a big meringue-covered piece from the end. "So," I said, "What are you doing here? I thought you were spending the holidays in Aruba or someplace."

He gave a small shrug. "I thought about it, but when the chance came up to spend Christmas with Mel, naturally I jumped on it."

"My mom dumped me on him," Melanie said, her eyes fixed on the screen of her tablet. "She's in Brazil on her honeymoon with some tennis dude."

I lifted an eyebrow. "Great hearing," I commented.

Miles kept his expression perfectly flat as he said, "Mel's mother can be a little impulsive." And the note of cheer he injected into his voice sounded forced as he added, "But it all worked out great for me. I don't get to spend nearly enough time with my girl."

I dug into the pie again. "How long are you staying?"

"A few days. We're on our way to see my mother in Myrtle Beach. I thought we'd check out the bunny slope at Far Heights, and I need to meet with some contractors while I'm here."

I said, "Wow. Skiing and the beach for Christmas. Lucky kid."

He cut into his first bite of pie. "Actually," he said, "it was supposed to be Aspen and St. Bart's, but I had already rented out my condo in Aspen for the holidays, and Mel's mother forgot to leave her passport with me. So it's going to be a low-key Christmas."

"You've got a condo in Aspen?"

He smiled. "And a beach house in the Virgin Islands."

And three ex-wives and a daughter. How many other things did I not know about him?

Not that it mattered. He wasn't *really* my boyfriend. We weren't really even officially dating. We were barely casual friends. Acquaintances at best.

My cell phone rang and I was glad. I fumbled to unzip my vest pocket and take it out.

"Where are you?" Buck asked without preamble.

I frowned at his abruptness, but knew it only meant he was under stress. I could hear the crackle of police radios in the background. "Still in town, why?"

"Listen, can you meet me at…" I could picture him consulting his notebook, "the entrance of the Heavenly

Homes trailer park? I need you to go with me on a compassionate call."

I blew out a breath. Since the Hanover County Sheriff's Department had lost its only female deputy–due to the fact that she preferred sleeping with my husband over working with him—those informal duties that were deemed to require a woman's touch had fallen to whomever Buck could snare. These usually involved female prisoners or minor children who, in Buck's opinion, would be put at ease by the presence of a woman. And to be fair, he did usually try to find someone who was at least on the county payroll—someone from DFACS or the Health Department, or occasionally even my Aunt Mart, who, as the wife of the retired sheriff, at least had plenty of experience.

On the other hand, part of my therapy dog work was as a volunteer crisis counselor, which usually meant showing up with my dog and staying quiet while traumatized children or victims of violent crime clung to Cisco and tried to believe in a world that would one day be normal again. Accompanying an officer to inform the family of a loved one's death was not exactly within the scope of my duties, but it wasn't entirely outside them either.

"I tried Peggy but she's on her way to the hospital to fill out the paperwork on that abandoned baby and everybody else is either still at the parade or out Christmas shopping," Buck went on. Peggy Miller was Hanover County's only licensed social worker, and she ran the Department of Family and Children's Services with a staff of four overworked and underpaid clerks. I could see where this was headed. "I've got to go tell a minor child that her daddy is dead and remove her from the home. It sure would be a lot easier on her if it wasn't a couple of policemen with guns she saw when she opened the door."

I groaned out loud, rubbing my forehead. Miles speared another piece of pie. I said, "Who is it?"

"The victim's Earl Lewis. The daughter's name is Ashleigh. Thirteen or fourteen, I think. Far as I can tell, no other relatives in the state. The mother died four or five years ago."

"I don't know them."

"No reason you should. He wasn't exactly what you'd call an outstanding citizen. That poor kid couldn't have had much of a home life, but I guess it was better than no home life at all."

Now you know why everyone likes Buck. He genuinely cares about other people. He knows how to put himself in their place. And when he says things like that, he puts me in my place too.

I sighed. "Okay. I'll stop by and pick up Cisco. It's out Highway 16, isn't it? Past the old cannery?"

"Yeah, just pull up beside the entrance sign, I'll lead you in."

I watched Miles eat the last bite of pie. "So what happened? Traffic accident?"

Buck hesitated just a moment. "Murder," he said. "He was stabbed in the throat."

I didn't spend a lot of time saying goodbye to Miles or to his ever-so-charming daughter. That was probably rude of me. And I'm really not certain what it says about me when I was relieved to trade the warm diner and coffee with an attractive man to rush to the aid of my ex-husband at a crime scene.

My house was on the way to the Heavenly Homes trailer park, and all three dogs came scrabbling to the front door when I pulled up—despite the fact that two of them were supposed to be securely crated behind a closed door. As I have told my students repeatedly, it's pointless to correct a dog for undesirable behavior after the fact, so I pretended not to notice that Mischief and Magic had once again let themselves out of their crates without permission. I turned all three dogs out into the yard briefly for a toilet break, settled the Aussies down with a chew bone, and grabbed Cisco's therapy dog vest from the front closet. Cisco looked from Mischief's chew bone to me with a hurt expression on his face until I opened the door and invited, "Okay, boy. Load up!" Then he dashed out into the dark, tail spinning like a propeller blade, and he was sitting beside the tail gate of the SUV with an excited grin on his face when I got there.

Cisco fogged up the back window with his breath while I made my way down the dark and almost deserted highway, looking for the sign that heralded the entrance to the trailer park. I would have missed it had I not seen the patrol car parked just inside the entrance, and I pulled in beside it, next to the wooden sign with the faded lettering that read, "Heavenly Homes." Buck put his car in gear and led the way down the gravel road.

The trailer park was one of those that had probably been a pretty good deal fifteen or twenty years ago. Most of the homes were double-wides, and the little squares of yard were not too close together. Behind front windows I could see the twinkle of Christmas tree lights, and some had even gone to the expense of decorating their roof lines and setting fluorescent snowmen in their front yards. Only a few of the drives were occupied by rusted-out cars on blocks, and one fellow with an obvious sense of humor had even strung a row of multi-colored Christmas lights around the open hood of his.

Buck pulled into the short dirt drive that led to a darkened double-wide at the end of the block. He got out and stood in that watchful manner that is second nature to every policeman, his hands resting on his utility belt, looking around. I opened the back of the SUV and gave Cisco a firm command to stay while I snapped on his vest and leash. I knew he obeyed only because he hadn't seen Buck yet.

I released Cisco and walked him up the drive toward the patrol car. The minute he saw Buck, he forgot everything he had ever known about heeling, and I knew I'd never get him back under control until the two of them had greeted each other. So when we were three feet away I gave up the struggle to keep him by my side and said, "Okay, release," as he dashed toward his hero. At least I got to pretend it was my idea.

I glanced around in the glow of the neighbor's Christmas lights while Buck bent down to rub Cisco's wriggling body, telling him what a fine fellow he was. The only cars in the drive were ours, and there wasn't a light on inside. It was barely eight o'clock, and I didn't think a teenager would be in bed already. I could hear the neighbor's television through the thin glass windows of the trailer but not a sound from the one in front of us.

"I don't think anyone's here," I said, unnecessarily.

"Yeah, looks like it." Buck straightened up and handed Cisco's leash to me.

"Maybe she got scared when her daddy didn't come home and went to a friend's house."

"Probably." He moved toward the front door and I followed, keeping Cisco close. "Might as well make sure."

He pushed the buzzer, which made no sound, then knocked on the sagging storm door. After a moment, he opened the storm door and knocked again, loudly, on the main door.

I kept my voice low, just in case someone was home. "Where did you find him?"

"Somebody spotted his truck down a gully off the old Switchback Road. His body was in the camper. I figure he'd been there less than a day, but in this weather it's hard to tell by guessing."

"Any idea who?"

"He wasn't the most popular guy when he was drinking. We're doing some interviews." Most of the violent crimes around here were either family disputes or drug and alcohol related, and they were fairly simple to resolve. Most of the time the perpetrator would be at home waiting for the deputies when they came to arrest him. On the other hand, crimes that weren't solved within the first twenty-four hours became exponentially harder to solve. I knew that Buck was counting on his deputies making an arrest tonight.

He knocked again. Again there was silence.

"Come on, let's check around back."

He turned on his flashlight to light our path as we rounded the dark corner of the trailer. There were a couple of overflowing trashcans, a pile of rotting lumber beside a metal storage shed, and a propane gas tank. The three wooden steps to the back door were too narrow for all of us, so I let Buck go up while Cisco and I waited. He knocked, and the door swung inward a few inches. He glanced down at me. I came up the steps behind him.

Buck pushed the door open and called, "Ashleigh? It's Sheriff Lawson. Are you here?"

He stepped inside the threshold, and because he had not brought me along for nothing, I added my woman's voice, "Ashleigh, it's okay. Don't be scared. We just want to talk to you."

But the trailer was clearly empty.

Buck moved his flashlight beam around the small kitchen until he found the light switch. He pressed it and a cluttered, untidy kitchen with faded brick-patterned linoleum and stained wallpaper came into view. There was a box of cereal on the table and crumbs scattered around. A loaf of bread was open on the counter. There were dishes in the sink.

Buck's brows drew together as he sniffed the air. "Do you smell bleach?"

"So? Someone did the laundry."

But his frown only deepened. "I don't know. Doesn't look to me like the housekeeper has been in today. Stay here," he said and moved toward the front of the house.

I heard him call out again, "Is anyone here? It's the police." And I sighed, glancing around. I don't always do what Buck tells me to—in fact, I almost never do—but it was pointless to follow him through an empty house.

There was a shelf above the greasy microwave that held a stack of mail, a small vase of plastic flowers, and a couple of framed photographs. I glanced through the mail, which consisted of two months' worth of telephone, electric and water bills, as well as a letter from Fidelity Mortgage which I could not imagine contained good news. I picked up a photograph of a man and woman in wedding attire. The frame was sticky with kitchen grime and the glass was dull. I turned it over and slipped the cheap cardboard backing up into the frame a little. On the back of the photograph someone had written "Amy and Earle, 6-22-89". I replaced the photograph and picked up the one next to it, a school photograph of a dark-haired young girl I assumed to be Ashleigh. Why did she look familiar to me?

While I had been nosing around I had let the leash go slack in my hand. A crackling sound distracted me, and I turned to see that Cisco had taken advantage of my preoccupation to put his front paws on the counter and help himself to the open loaf of bread.

I don't usually yell at my dogs, but counter-surfing—especially someone else's counter, in someone else's house—was a *huge* No-No, and every dog I had ever trained knew it. I took a deep breath and bellowed at the top of my lungs, "*Cisco, wrong!*"

I had intended to startle him, and that was exactly what I did. He dropped from the counter and scooted across the room with such force that he jerked the leash from my hand, lost traction on the slippery floors, and slid the last few feet across the linoleum on his butt. His momentum was stopped by a wooden door, which popped open a few inches when he hit it. He sat there, grinning at me sheepishly, and it was hard not to laugh back.

Buck called, "Hey, what's going on?"

"We're okay!" I called back and went to collect Cisco. For good measure, I muttered under my breath as sternly as I could, "You rotten dog. You know better."

I bent to retrieve Cisco's leash and knew immediately I had found the source of the bleach smell.

I nudged the door all the way open and peeked inside. I expected a laundry room, but when I turned on the light I realized it was a bathroom. The first thing I noticed was a smear of blood on the yellowing white tile of the floor. The second thing I noticed was that the tub was filled with water, what appeared to be bed sheets, and a great quantity of bleach. The water was pink.

I closed my eyes briefly and swallowed hard, hoping this didn't mean what I thought it meant. Buck came up behind me and surveyed the scene silently for a moment. Then he said, "Damn."

He took out his radio and called for backup.

SEVEN

The Hanover County Sheriff's Department had twelve deputies, and Buck pulled six of them off parade and traffic control duties to conduct door-to-door interviews of the neighbors while he and Deke secured the trailer as a crime scene. All of this activity naturally drew some attention, and it wasn't long before a cluster of neighbors, many of them with coats thrown over their pajamas, was gathered in the tiny yard.

Cisco and I sat on the front stoop, out of the way of the investigators, as ordered, but standing by in case we were needed to help conduct a search in the field that surrounded the trailer park, also as ordered. It would have been warmer in the car, but I didn't want to be that far away from the action. And since very few people can resist coming up to pet a waggy-tailed golden retriever, I was in a good position to keep up with what was going on.

My phone rang two or three times, but when I looked at the caller ID, it was only Miles. It wasn't that I didn't want to talk to him, exactly, but this wasn't the time or the place. And there was absolutely nothing he had to say to me that was more important, or more interesting, than what was going on here. Finally I turned my phone off, and I only felt a little guilty about it.

"Hey, is this a drug dog?" someone wanted to know. "I heard ol' Earle was up to some pretty sneaky stuff, but I didn't know it was drugs."

I explained that Cisco was not a drug dog, but a search dog. "What kind of sneaky stuff?" I wanted to know.

The original man shrugged and wandered away, and someone else said, "Aw, he wasn't such a bad sort. Just fell on hard times is all."

"A man that hung out with the kind of trash he did was bound to get hisself offed sooner or later," observed a middle-aged woman in a pink fleece bathrobe, puffing hard on a cigarette. "No better than he deserved, if you ask me."

"Now, Ellie," said another woman with a note of reprimand in her voice, "he wasn't so bad when he wasn't drinking. And he was purely devoted to his wife. It just about tore him apart when she died. That's what started him on the downhill if you ask me." She reached down to scratch Cisco's head. "What a sweet dog. They don't let us have pets here."

I said, "What did his wife die of?"

"Cancer, I think." She straightened up. "He kept her wedding band on a chain that hung from his rearview mirror in his truck. He gave me a ride into town one day when my car broke down on the side of the road and when I said something about it he told me he started every day by kissing that ring for good luck. Now, you can't tell me a man like that is all bad."

Something stirred in my memory, and I frowned a little. "You wouldn't happen to know if there was engraving inside the ring, would you?"

She shook her head. "I couldn't tell. What do you suppose happened to the girl?"

Another woman said, "Somebody said they saw her go off with her boyfriend somewhere this afternoon."

I said, "Excuse me," and stood up. My back side was practically frozen from sitting on the cold concrete steps. "I need to find out how long I'm supposed to wait. Cisco, let's go."

The front door had been sealed off with crime scene tape, so I went around to the back. The back door was open and all the lights were on inside, but there was a strip of police tape across the opening of it as well. Deputies managed to go in and out by ducking under, but I knew better than to try the same thing. Forensics units tend to take a dim view of dog hair all over their crime scenes. I stood on the ground at the edge of the steps, which put my head about even with the threshold of the door and called, "Hey, Buck!"

In a minute he came to the door, looking busy and preoccupied. "Yeah, you can go on home, Raine. We've got three people who said she left in a blue or green Chevy this afternoon, and that she had a duffle bag with her. We might be looking at a runaway, so we're going to follow up on some leads before we declare her missing."

I said, "I need to ask you something."

Someone inside said, "Buck, you got a minute?"

He glanced over his shoulder, and then back at me, trying to hide his mild annoyance. "Okay, but make it quick, will you?"

He ducked under the tape and came down the steps. A couple of deputies were poking around the wood pile and searching the area around it with their flashlights, and his gaze flickered toward them. "Y'all take down that wood pile piece by piece and lay it out," Buck called. "And check out that storage shed. We've got a warrant."

"What are you looking for?" I asked.

"The murder weapon, maybe. There's a knife missing from the stand on the counter, and we didn't see it anywhere in the house."

"Did you look in the dishwasher?" I suggested.

He looked at me for a moment, then walked back to the door and said something to one of the men inside. I felt smug. Buck looked impatient when he returned. "Was there something you wanted, Raine?"

"Hey, it's not like I'm having a great time standing out here in the cold either, you know." And for a moment I was so irritated I almost turned and stalked away. "I could be at home watching *It's a Wonderful Life*."

He tried, not very successfully, to look apologetic. His eyes kept wandering to the boys with the flashlights. "Sorry. I didn't mean to keep you out here so long. What did you want to ask?"

I hesitated. The whole thing sounded a little farfetched now that I said it out loud, "Did you guys find Lewis's wedding ring on a chain hanging from the rearview mirror of his truck?"

For the first time, I had his attention. "Not that I know of. How come?"

"Because his wife's name was Amy, and someone said he kept his wedding ring on a chain hanging from his mirror. And tonight I was in the diner and this guy in front of me—a strange fellow dressed in camo with a kind of crazy look in his eyes—he dropped a wedding ring that was engraved *Forever, Amy* inside. He had a big buck knife on his belt and blood all over his jacket. I just thought it was a coincidence, the names and all."

Buck stared at me.

"Hey, Sheriff!" The guys had opened the shed door and were shining their lights inside.

"Stay here," Buck said tersely. "Don't move." And he hurried across the narrow strip of dirt yard to the shed.

Well, I didn't go far—just far enough to see that what the deputies had uncovered was a shed filled with flat screen TV's, laptop computers, stereos, smart phones, and MP3 players, among other things, many of them still in their boxes. There was also a couple of pairs of skis, an outboard motor, two generators, and enough power tools—all still sealed in boxes—to open a woodworking shop.

"Looks like Santa Claus got here a little early," one of the guys observed.

And somebody else agreed, "I guess we cracked our burglary ring."

"And found a motive for murder," Buck said.

Buck took my statement about the man in the diner, and took another statement from the woman who had told me about the wedding ring. He sent Deke back into town to interview Lucy, who had gotten a much better look at Camo Man than I had.

"Do you think it might really be something?" I asked, both excited and a little worried by the possibility. To think I had stood that close to a cold-blooded killer—and had even given him a quarter—was a little unsettling, to say the least. Knowing that he was still out there somewhere was even worse.

"Could be." Buck was writing in his notebook. "We'll search the truck again for the ring. But it's pretty clear Earl was involved in these burglaries we've been trying to track down, and if he had a partner, and if they had some kind of disagreement that went bad…" He gave a small lift of one shoulder without looking up. "Somebody tried to mop up an awful lot of blood with those bed sheets that were in the tub, and we know the body was moved from wherever he was killed to the back of the truck. A hunting knife would match the wound."

"And the girl? Do you think she's okay?'

He snapped the notebook closed. "We won't know until we find her. Listen, Raine, I've gotta go. We'll be up all night cataloguing this stuff and I've still got a lot of people to talk to. See you later, okay?" He was walking away before he finished speaking.

"You're welcome," I called after him.

Buck, of course, did not look back.

The minute I parked in front of my house I knew something was amiss. All the downstairs lights were on, and even if I had accidentally left the front lights on in my hurry to leave, I hadn't even been in the kitchen, and I could see the light from the kitchen window spreading a pool over the side yard. I could smell wood smoke faintly, and though I did like to keep a fire going in the woodstove in the kitchen, I was almost certain it had gone out long before I left to take Santa Dog on his first therapy visit. I went up the steps and opened the door cautiously, Cisco swishing his tail excitedly beside me. The sound of the television reached me from the living room. I called uncertainly,

"Mischief?" How in the world had she learned to work the remote control?

I heard the sound of paws hitting the floor and Mischief and Magic came trotting out of the living room, grinning happily, and were met in the hallway by Miles Young, who came from the kitchen with a glass of wine in his hand. My mouth fell open in astonishment.

"Before you say anything," he said and seemed surprised that I didn't interrupt him. He went on, "I must have called you six times. Is your phone broken? And we waited almost an hour in the car. Your door was open so…."

"You did not." I found my voice at last, and my outrage bubbled up. "You did *not* just walk into my house and make yourself at home! This is over the line, Miles, and I mean it. I can't believe you would do such a thing."

"I told you she would be mad," sang girl's voice from the living room.

"She's not mad, honey, she's just surprised," Miles called back. To me he said, with deliberate emphasis, "I told her people did things differently in the country. I told her they were more neighborly."

I thought my eyes would pop out of my head with things I couldn't say in front of a child.

The Aussies wriggled and pressed up against me and I petted them absently. Cisco sat hopefully in front of Miles and he produced a dog biscuit from his pocket. It was easy to see how he wouldn't have had any trouble getting past my faithful guard dogs. He never made an appearance without a pocketful of dog biscuits and he had trained them well.

He pressed the glass of wine in my hand. "I hope you like white," he said. "It's all I had left. I figured you'd need it after the night you've had. Come on in the kitchen," he urged. "I made a fire. Let me explain."

Unfortunately for him, I was not quite so well trained. I stared at him with clenched jaw.

"She's mad," Melanie called over the sound of the television.

"No, she's not."

"Yes, she is," I muttered, low enough so that hopefully only he could hear.

He said, "I brought pie. Meg had another one in the back."

Damn him, anyway.

I followed him down the hall to the kitchen, past the living room where Melanie had made herself at home on the sofa with a bag of chips and a cola and was watching some vampire show on TV. The dogs hesitated when they saw the little girl and the chips, but they calculated the odds and decided their best bet was the kitchen, with us. Or perhaps they understood the word "pie".

My kitchen is one of the big old-fashioned types, with a wood burning stove on the center wall, and a door that can close it off from the rest of the house. I smelled coffee and wood smoke, and it was pleasantly cozy, which infuriated me. I closed the door and turned to Miles, fuming.

"Five seconds," I said.

"No heat, frozen pipes, carbon monoxide poisoning," he replied, deadpan. "I tried every motel in town. The nearest vacancy is Asheville. It's ten o'clock, the overpasses are icy, I thought you'd be home. I left six messages."

I exploded in a hiss, "Are you kidding me? You're in charge of multi-billion dollar building projects and you can't even defrost a frozen water pipe?"

His eyes grew cool. "Darlin'," he said, "I can re-plumb that entire house with garden hose and silicone caulk if I have to, but I'd prefer not to do it while my daughter's lips are turning blue."

I spun away, drew a breath, and took a sip of the wine. It tasted expensive. Damn him, anyway.

He crossed the room and poured a cup of coffee. The dogs' claws clicked on the wood floors as they hopefully searched for treats. I felt like a cad.

But I had also been a dog trainer for fifteen years and I knew the importance of boundaries. And I knew when mine had been violated. I said, "You shouldn't have come in here without permission."

He turned, leaning against the counter with one of my coffee mugs cupped in his hand. "I understand. But if it had been Maude or Buck or Sonny who was in trouble and needed shelter, would you still be mad?"

I said, sputtering a little, "That's different."

"Why?"

"Because they're –" I knew how that sentence ended and stopped it before I could embarrass myself further.

He supplied for me, "Friends." He sipped his coffee, watching me. "I thought we were past that. Guess not."

He put the coffee cup on the counter and started for the living room.

"Where are you going?"

"Asheville."

"But the overpasses are icy."

"Right."

"Wait."

I couldn't believe I was saying it, and I had absolutely no choice. He turned to me and I looked at him, angry and frustrated and helpless and resigned. There is no worse feeling in the world than knowing you have things to talk about, but not knowing how to say them. All I could manage was, "You don't just get to have everything you want, Miles. You've got to respect people's boundaries."

He said nothing. He just waited.

After a moment I said, grudgingly, "I only have one guest room. You'll have to sleep on the couch."

"Thank you." And he smiled. He was incredibly charming when he smiled, and my willpower was not what it used to be. "May I kiss you now?"

"No."

Of course I was hoping he would try to change my mind, and he wouldn't have had to try very hard. But he just gave a little shrug, winked at me, and left the room.

Damn him, anyway.

EIGHT

I slept restlessly and woke before dawn, creeping around so as not to disturb my guests. I hate having strangers sleep over in my house. I'd had to lock all three dogs in my bedroom with me, and Mischief and Magic had taken turns trying to see who could jump on my bed and land lightly enough at my feet that I wouldn't notice. This of course insulted Cisco, who knew perfectly well dogs were not allowed on my bed, and he felt it his sworn duty to make sure I knew whenever an infraction occurred. We played this game for almost an hour before Mischief and Magic were finally convinced they could not get away with anything. When I awoke in the morning, who should be curled up on either side of my feet but two Australian shepherds. Cisco, with his head on his paws, was eyeing me reproachfully from his bed in the corner.

I chased the dogs off the bed and scolded them in a whisper, which is hardly an effective way to scold a dog at all, but I couldn't risk waking up our company.

I also could not go downstairs without brushing my teeth and running a comb through my curly brown hair, which had grown longer than I liked over the past few months. I spent far too long looking for the bathrobe without a stain on it. I really hate having strangers in my house.

The dogs came clattering down the stairs despite my shushing, and when I glanced into the living room I saw the blankets had been folded and neatly stacked with the pillow. I smelled coffee from the kitchen.

My yellow kitchen was cozy and warm with the flames from the glass doors of the wood stove reflected on the glossy sealed surface of the pine floors and dancing off the copper pots that hung from the rack over the stove. It was still pitch-black outside, and the one hanging lamp over the breakfast table that Miles had turned on gave the room a hushed, intimate feel. It reminded me of the mornings when I used to get up before dawn to ride up the mountain with my daddy to cut a Christmas tree, bouncing over the rutted dirt logging roads in a beat-up pickup truck he kept only for farm work. We would spend all morning searching for just the perfect tree, then haul it back home to arrive just as Mother was taking a pan of sticky buns out of the oven. I was filled unexpectedly with a warm glow of nostalgia, and when Miles turned he saw me smiling.

"Well, that's nice," he said, lifting his cup to me. "After last night I wasn't sure you'd ever smile at me again."

I shrugged and followed the dogs into the kitchen, finding it hard to remember to be annoyed with him at this hour. "I was just thinking about Christmas. I've got to get a tree."

The dogs milled about his feet briefly, saw that he didn't have any treats, and then raced to the door. I let them out into the back yard, and a wave of cold lingered when I shut the door again. Miles handed me a cup of coffee.

"Do you really do the whole Christmas thing, with a tree and lights and stockings over the fireplace?"

"Sure." I was surprised. "Don't you?"

He shrugged. "I don't really celebrate Christmas."

I stared at him, warming my hands around the coffee mug. "Why not? I mean—are you Jewish or something?"

He looked amused. "No. Would it make a difference if I were?"

I was thoroughly embarrassed and felt it to the tips of my toes. "No." Great. It wasn't even seven o'clock in the morning and already we were off to a bad start. "It's just that –you've got a daughter, a mother with a beach house, three ex-wives, and a condo in Aspen," I blurted. "I'm just wondering what else I don't know about you."

He regarded me mildly as he sipped his coffee. "They have something to fix that these days. It's called Google."

I was momentarily nonplussed. What kind of world did he live in, where people Googled potential boyfriends? I frowned a little into my coffee and muttered, "Well, you know us mountain folk. We don't put much faith in that new-fangled technology."

By the way he looked at me, I could tell he wasn't sure if I was kidding. I was, by the way. Mostly.

But Google? Seriously?

He said, "Christmas is for kids, and when you grow up with an alcoholic father you don't have a lot of childhood memories you want to re-create. Besides, my ex always has Melanie for Christmas, and I never had anyone to celebrate with."

I tried again, determined to hold on to some semblance of the Christmas spirit. "I'm sorry I was a grouch last night."

"That's okay. I overstepped." That smile again. Damn, what he could do to me with that smile.

And then the smile faded. "No excuse, but it's been kind of a stressful week. This whole thing with Mel took me by surprise. I shouldn't have made it your problem. But we'll be out of your hair in no time. I'm going to go over to the house and see if I can figure out what went wrong with the heat pump, and get a plumber out there at first light."

While his designer home was being built on the top of my mountain, Miles was temporarily living in a luxury-model mobile home with granite countertops, a wrap around deck, hot tub, and two bathrooms, each one bigger than my bedroom. His temporary quarters were situated at the entry gate of his resort community, which made it very convenient for supervising the construction. It also was almost within walking distance of my house.

Sipping my coffee, I said, "I'll tell you what went wrong with the heat pump. It iced over. We've had nights in the teens since you've been gone. You should have winterized."

His brows drew together sharply and he swore softly under his breath. "You're probably right," he admitted in a moment. "I didn't plan to be gone so long, but then this business came up with Mel. . . Who knew it would get that cold this early, anyway?"

"It doesn't usually," I admitted. "If you had let me know, I could have checked on it for you."

He unknotted his brow with a visible effort. "Thanks, hon, but I have people who were supposed to be doing that."

Right. His people.

I heard a scrabbling at the door and went to let the dogs in. They flowed around us, butts wiggling, faces grinning. Miles obligingly reached down to scratch ears and chins. "Sorry, guys," he said, "all out of treats. Hit me later."

"Dogs," I commanded sharply, because they were starting to be pests. "Settle." I pointed to the corner of the kitchen, and one by one, with unhappy looks, they filed over to their places. When Cisco looked as though he thought he might be the exception to the rule, I raised an eyebrow and made a "Nuh!" sound in the back of my throat. Reluctantly, he flopped down with his head on his paws.

All right, then. Rarely did I get a chance to show off what a good dog trainer I was. Usually, I just got to show off my expertise at rescuing myself from some disaster my dogs had created. The morning was looking up.

Miles was making an effort too. He said, "So tell me about your case. Who did you and Cisco rescue last night?"

Cisco's ears lifted hopefully at the sound of his name, then lowered when no command was forthcoming. I said, "No one, actually. It was kind of a false alarm, but interesting." It was nice of him to ask, but as I summarized the events of the night before I couldn't help feeling anxious about the missing girl. I wondered whether Buck had found her by now and what kind of life would be waiting for her now that her father was gone. I was abruptly depressed again.

When I was finished, Miles said, "Do you mind if I make an observation?" Apparently it didn't matter whether I did or not, because he went on, "Last month you were dealing with a serial killer and a skeleton in your back yard. The month before that you were tied up and left to burn to death in your own building by a psychopath. Now you walk in on a murder scene and don't even blink an eye. I'm starting to think this little corner of the Smoky Mountains is not quite the paradise I was led to believe."

I smiled sweetly. "Oops," I said.

His eyes twinkled, and for a moment we were all right again.

But I sobered. "I'm really kind of worried. If it was that guy I saw in the diner, and if the girl was there when he broke in…"

"Then the neighbors wouldn't have seen her leaving that afternoon," Miles reminded me. He was always so rational about these things.

"I suppose," I admitted. "Still, I think I'll call the office as soon as the day shift gets in."

"Or," suggested Miles, "you could wait until someone calls you. As in, when they need your help."

I had to bite my tongue. He really didn't get the way things worked around here. And he sounded a little too much, at that moment, like my ex-husband.

The silence was awkward for a beat or two, and then Miles nodded toward the back yard. "How's the construction project?"

I sighed. "Expensive. Looks like we're shut down until I can figure out how to pay for this thing."

The truth was that I had Miles to thank for the progress that had been made so far. He had sent his top crew down to reconstruct my building, even though it meant pulling them off his own project. I would have felt even worse about not being able to finish the construction if I hadn't been sure the crew would still have jobs to go to with Miles.

"Looks like they've got you under roof, anyway."

"Yeah, but no plumbing, HVAC, or kennel runs. I'm going to have to come up with something pretty soon or we'll be out of business."

"You're losing money every day you're closed."

"Tell me about it."

I could see the determination forming in his eyes that had laid waste to business opponents across the globe and every muscle in my body tensed. "Raine, I can send down a crew that will have you up and running before Christmas."

"No. I told you, I'm out of money. "

"Consider it a loan. Low interest, I'll draw up papers."

"No. I'm in more debt than I can afford already."

"An investment, then. "

"I already have a partner. Don't need another one."

"Damn it, Raine—"

"No."

"It's Christmas! Learn how to accept a gift, won't you?"

"A gift!" My outrage rose and it showed in my voice. "A gift is perfume or jewelry or—or—fruit of the month! Not a ten thousand dollar construction renovation that I already told you I can't afford. You can't just *buy* people, Miles. Boundaries, for heaven's sake!"

We glared at each other for a moment and I could see he was trying as hard as I was not to say what he was thinking. His nostrils flared with a breath. My fingers tightened around my coffee cup. Neither of us would be the first to blink. Finally he muttered, "You are the stubbornest person I have ever met."

"Said the pot to the kettle." But I allowed my shoulders to relax fractionally as I took a sip of my coffee.

My relationship with Miles is complicated, to say the least. First of all, we are sworn enemies when it comes to his development project; he has decided not to let that fact bother him, and I am coming to an uneasy peace with it, myself. And there is an awful lot I like about him. You always know where you stand with Miles; ask him anything and he'll tell you the truth. He's completely comfortable in his own skin. He makes me laugh. When he comes to dinner, he not only cooks, but he does the dishes. He is at home wherever he is. I like his unself-conscious affection, which he extends as easily to me as he does to my dogs—even though I wish he wouldn't be quite so affectionate in public. And one cold, rainy night not long ago, he had stayed up till dawn helping me search the woods for a lost dog. No one asked him to. He had just done it. There's a lot to like about him.

But he can also be controlling, abrupt, determined, stubborn and a little arrogant. Since I am also most of those things—except arrogant—we have a tendency to butt heads a lot. To Miles's credit, he's usually the first one to make an attempt to smooth things over.

He regarded me silently for another moment. Then he said, "You know, it would be a lot easier to respect your boundaries if I actually knew what they were. We're more than neighbors but not quite friends. Or maybe more than friends but not quite lovers. I can't kiss you in public but can I kiss you in private?" He shrugged. "Anybody's guess. A few clear signals wouldn't be unwelcome here."

My muscles stiffened again. "Look, Miles…"

He held up a hand. "It's okay. I know you have some things to work out. Patience is one of my many virtues. But while you're thinking about it, consider this: I am going to be in your life. There's no avoiding that. I can be your enemy, or your friend, or your lover. You choose."

There was that strange, silly fluttering in the vicinity of my ribcage again, and the heat that crawled up my throat. He had fabulous eyes. Sometimes I just couldn't stop looking at them. I said, "You don't have an opinion?"

"I do," he conceded gravely. "But I wouldn't want to accidentally violate your boundaries by expressing it."

As hard as I tried, I couldn't fight the smile that tugged at a corner of my lips. I tried to hide it by lifting my coffee cup. He smiled back at me. We were comfortable for a moment.

I searched for a neutral topic. "Melanie seems like a smart girl." I probably should have said *nice* or *sweet* but couldn't quite manage it.

"She is." But his expression was troubled again as he looked into his coffee cup. "She doesn't like me much. Hates being here. Who can blame her? I've seen her maybe three times in two years. I don't know anything about her life. What do nine-year-old girls like, anyway?"

I was appalled. My collie Majesty had been living with my Aunt Mart for less than a month and if I didn't see her at least every other day I started to go into withdrawal. How could a father see his own child only three times in two years? I tried to keep my opinions to myself. "I don't know. I was never a little girl. I was a tomboy. I liked dogs and mountain bikes. I was a junior handler at thirteen. You know, if you spent more time with her you'd probably know exactly what she likes to do." Ah well, I knew I wouldn't be able to keep my opinions to myself very long. But it was worth a try.

Miles, of course, was unruffled. He always was. "You mean," he corrected, "if she spent more time with me. I make plans to pick her up every weekend of the year and for a month in the summer— she always has something she would rather do. Her mother has her in this fancy boarding school in New York and she has her friends..." He shrugged. "She was supposed to be skiing in Austria this Christmas. Hell of a thing, huh, when spending Christmas with your dad is a punishment?"

I wanted to say something. I had no idea what.

He took a final sip of coffee and set the cup aside. "Well, I'd better wake her up so we can get going."

"What—now?" I looked out the window. "It's still dark. What are you going to do, just make her sit and wait while you work?"

"We'll go into town for breakfast. It'll be light by the time we get back."

What was wrong with me? I didn't like kids; I had no idea what to do with one. I couldn't believe what I was about to say. Blame it on Christmas.

I said, "Come on, Miles. She's had a hard couple of days. Let her sleep. I'll bring her over when she wakes up."

He looked at me with a kind of amused skepticism. "Are you sure? She can be kind of a handful."

I shrugged, suddenly not so sure. "Okay, I'm not saying I have the greatest maternal instincts, but I think I can handle a nine-year-old for an hour or two."

About that time I looked down and noticed that Cisco had managed to scoot himself, an inch at a time, across the kitchen floor, until he now lay only a few feet from us, head on paws, just as though he thought he could convince me that was where I had left him. I fixed him with a glare.

Here is the thing about teaching the "stay": you give a dog an inch, and he will take a mile. Dogs are incredibly precise about these things, and the first time you allow him to get away with moving even a foot or two out of position, you have taught him that he gets to determine *where* he should stay. It's almost never a good idea to let dogs start negotiating with humans over territory.

My dogs know when I put them somewhere, they are to stay exactly there until I tell them differently.

And of course they keep trying to find out whether or not I really mean it.

My eyes widened dramatically and Cisco's ears flattened. I said, in a very low, quietly menacing tone that was reserved for only the worst training infractions, "Where do you belong?" I pointed a sharp finger in his direction. "Shame on you! Go! Back to your place! Now!"

Cisco scrambled back to his place with the other two dogs, and Miles laughed. "Okay, maybe you can. I'll probably be back before she wakes up anyway, but she's got her cell phone if she needs to call me. Thanks, Raine." He put his coffee mug in the sink and caressed my cheek lightly—in lieu of a kiss, I guessed—on the way out.

I smiled and waved to him and then released the dogs to their breakfasts, feeling a little better about things between us. Then I took my coffee to the study where my computer was set up and called up Google.

I was still scrolling through the myriad web pages relating to Miles Young, his various enterprises, his various holding companies, his various charitable activities, his various newspaper appearances, his various lawsuits—both as complainant and defendant—his various feature magazine articles, his various supermodel-type girlfriends and even his Wikipedia entry when Sonny called. "Have you heard anything more about the abandoned baby?" she wanted to know.

"Only what I knew when I left last night. I'm going to give Rita a call in a few minutes and see if anything turned up." Rita was the day dispatcher, and if she wasn't too busy she could often save me the trouble—and awkwardness—of going to Buck or one of his deputies for the information I needed. And, being a woman, she was on my side about the divorce. "I doubt it's a very high priority right now, though." Briefly, I told her about Earl Lewis's murder. "And the worst part is," I added, "I might have been standing behind the man who did it in the diner. Apparently Earl was involved in some kind of burglary ring and Buck thinks this guy might have been a partner who thought Earl was cheating him or something."

"I don't know why these kinds of things always seem worse at Christmas," she said sadly. "As though we expect even the bad guys to be held to a higher standard this time of year."

"They think he might have been killed at home, then moved to the back of his truck. The truck was driven into a gully in the woods. The guys were still looking for his teenage daughter last night when I left."

"Somehow, the day looked a lot cheerier to me before I called you."

"Sorry." I reached for my coffee cup. "So how did the rest of the night go at the living Nativity? How was Mystery?"

"Perfect," Sonny said, and she did sound a little more cheerful at the mention of her dog's name. "But she's been pacing the floor all morning wanting to get back to them. I don't know how I can put up with this for the next two weeks."

"Put her out with the rest of the flock," I advised. "All she wants is to be doing her job."

"I know. That's what she keeps saying. But I'm half afraid she'll try to run into town and herd the other sheep home. She's very stubborn about some things."

Sonny had been known to give her animals too much credit, but in Mystery's case I wasn't so quick to dismiss her concerns. Sonny had come to own Mystery in the first place because Mystery had recognized Sonny's newly-purchased flock of sheep as the one she had used to herd.

I said, changing the subject, "Did you know Miles Young has a Wikipedia entry?"

"No, but it doesn't surprise me. He used to own that hockey team, you know."

"I do now." My voice sounded a little morose. "He showed up here last night. With his daughter." I waited to see if that would surprise her, but she said nothing. "He didn't have any heat in his house. I let them stay over."

"That was nice of you." She was carefully neutral on the subject of Miles Young, as well she should be. She was the lawyer for the citizen's action group—of which I was a member—that was aligned against him and his development project. She also knew that my relationship with the opposition, namely Miles, had gotten complicated over the past couple of months, and on that subject she generally did more listening than talking.

"Not really," I said, clicking another page. "I was kind of cranky about it."

I thought she smothered a chuckle. "Listen, Raine, what I called about was to tell you that I'm going to have to bow out of Christmas dinner with your aunt. I'll call her this afternoon and apologize. My sister cancelled her trip to Europe so I'll be going to Charleston to spend the holidays with her after all. I may even stay through January. She has a guest house so I can bring the dogs, and Winston Jones and his wife said they could house-sit and look after the farm animals."

"Wow. Sounds great." I hoped my words didn't sound as hollow as they felt. I had counted on Sonny at the Christmas table to take some of the awkwardness away from my first Christmas without Buck. Though Buck and I had been estranged for several years, off and on, and had even been briefly divorced once before, we had always put aside our differences for occasions like weddings, funerals and Christmas. I knew my aunt and uncle would miss him too, but with company present I had hoped they wouldn't talk about it.

"We'll miss you at Christmas," I added quickly, because I was afraid she would start to sense my disappointment. "But I'm glad you're going to get to be with your family. Let me know what you decide to do about January, and you know if you need anyone to check on things while you're gone, I have four- wheel drive."

We chatted for a few more minutes, and I disconnected, still browsing web pages then started punching out the numbers for the sheriff's office. It was eight forty-five and I was still in my pajamas, still drinking coffee, still fooling around on the computer and still not accomplishing much at all. I felt a stirring of guilt that I quickly squelched. I used to be much more ambitious. Since we had closed down the kennel—okay, since the divorce, if I'm completely honest—I hadn't been quite as energetic as I used to be. The dogs' training programs had suffered, and I'd put on a pound or two as a result—neither one of which would serve me well come spring when the competitive agility season began. I kept promising myself I was going to get back on track, but somehow never found the motivation. Maybe after Christmas.

The phone had just started to ring when I heard happy scrambling dog paws bounding into the room and a petulant voice demanded, "Where is my iPad?"

I quickly shut down the web page, disconnected, and spun around. Mischief, Magic and Cisco were happily winding themselves around a very tousled and unhappy looking Melanie, and she was ignoring them. I said first, "Cisco, Mischief, Magic, leave." They came over to me for the petting that was their due, and I rubbed them down dutifully. "Good morning, Melanie. How did you sleep?"

"My iPad," she repeated deliberately, "is missing."

I was determined to remain pleasant. "I'm sure it's around here somewhere. Your dad went over to the house to try to get the heat back on. I'll take you over after breakfast. What would you like?"

She replied ominously, "My iPad."

I could tell it was going to be a long morning.

I made a breakfast of canned fruit and dry oatmeal for the princess, who could not have eggs, dairy, wheat products, or nuts (but apparently had no problem with chips and cola), and she pushed it around sullenly in the bowl while she watched me clean up the kitchen. Cisco lay worshipfully at her feet, waiting for the dropped crumbs that always came from children. "If you don't find my iPad my mom will sue you," Melanie informed me.

"Good for her." I scrubbed hard at an imaginary stain on the tile.

"It cost a lot of money. "

"I'm sure it did."

"More than you probably even have."

"I wouldn't doubt that for a minute."

"This stuff is crap."

I ignored that until I heard a suspicious slurping sound from the vicinity of the table. I whirled and lunged to snatch the bowl she was holding out for Cisco before he could eat the entire bowl of fruit. "Don't," I told her darkly, "feed my dogs."

She scowled at me. "My mom says only trashy, low-class people keep dogs in their house."

I calmly scraped the remnants of her breakfast into the trash. "The queen of England would disagree with her. So would Oprah Winfrey. So would..." And while I tried to think of a celebrity who would actually impress her, the phone rang. I snatched it up gratefully.

"How's it going?" Miles inquired.

"Just great." I determined to keep my voice cheerful. "A little problem with a missing iPad but nothing I can't handle. We're just going to get cleaned up and head over your way. How's everything over there?"

"A pretty big mess." He did not sound happy. "We're waiting for a part for the heat pump, and they're going to have to tear out a wall in the living room and re-tile the master bath. It's a waste of money for a modular home. I should just have them haul it off and bring in a new one."

"Is that my dad?" Melanie demanded. "Tell him I want to go home!"

I turned my back on her, shielding the phone. "But you are going to be able to get the water back on today, right?" I tried not to sound too anxious.

"And by home I mean my real home!" Melanie added belligerently.

"Oh, sure. We'll have water by noon. Is that Mel in the background?"

"Yeah, she says 'Hi.'" And because I was afraid he was going to ask to speak to her—or worse—ask me to keep her a little while longer, I added quickly, "We'll see you in a little bit. Bye."

I turned to Melanie with the same kind of false enthusiasm with which I'd addressed her father. "All-righty, then. Are you ready to see your dad's place? Hurry up and get your things together and I'll drive you over."

She said, "Wait until I tell my dad you lost my iPad. See how much he likes you then."

I managed to hold on to my pleasant disposition. "Why don't you check under your pillow and in your backpack? I'll bet you just put it somewhere and forgot."

"I know you're only trying to impress my dad, and it's not going to work. You're not even his type."

I was fast losing my sunny smile. "You might try making your bed," I suggested. "Your iPad could be tangled up in the covers somewhere."

"I," she informed me archly, "don't make beds."

Right. She probably had people for that.

I stopped smiling. "Did you ever hear that story about Santa Claus making his list and checking it twice?"

She rolled her eyes. "You're pathetic." And she stalked away.

The missing iPad was located as I was putting Mischief into her crate and happened to notice something hard under her cushion. I drew it out with a wince, quickly polished off the dog hair and slobber, and scolded Mischief in a hiss, "Don't you ever do anything like that again!"

She looked at me as though she had no idea what I was talking about and settled down on her cushion with a huff. I looked guiltily over my shoulder as I straightened up, hoping there was no permanent damage, then called out cheerfully, "Melanie! Found your iPad."

NINE

Cisco looked at me hopefully as I opened the front door, and because I thought it might be nice to have someone along for the ride who actually knew how to pretend to be interested in what I had to say, I told him, "Okay, load up." He bounded through the door and Melanie, once more connected to her precious electronic tablet, trundled after him.

The morning was brisk and bright, with a white winter sun casting pale shadows through the spindly branches of naked trees. The layered mountains ranged in tone from sepia to lavender to phthalo blue, and I thought again about Christmas tree-hunting with my dad, the smell of evergreen and the bite of frost. I glanced at Melanie as I opened the back door of the SUV for Cisco and realized how sad it was for a little girl not to have those kinds of memories of her father. I felt slightly more kindly disposed toward her until she watched me fasten Cisco into his harness and seat belt, and she commented contemptuously, "A seat belt for a dog? That's stupid."

She flung herself into the passenger seat and slammed the door. I walked around to the driver's side without a word. I started the engine and waited, fixing her with my silent gaze, until she favored me with another one of her elaborate eye rolls and jerked her seat belt into its snapped position. I put the car in gear and started down the driveway, humming "We Wish You a Merry Christmas" under my breath. Melanie inserted her ear buds and fixed her eyes on the screen of her iPad.

My house is set well back from the highway in the shelter of the mountain, with a gravel driveway that's a little under a quarter of a mile long. There is a slight curve to it, so while I can't see the highway from the house, I can usually see anyone who is coming down my driveway long before they reach me. My mailbox is at the end of the driveway, and that was where, as I slowed to make my turn, I noticed a cardboard box sitting on the ground.

My postman always brings boxes to the house, and if I'm not home, he leaves them on the porch. So does UPS. So do all the reputable delivery services, which is why I thought, when I first glanced at it, that the box had probably blown off the back of someone's truck on the way to the dump. It did look a little battered and seemed to be held together with duct tape.

From the backseat, Cisco barked. Barking in the car was definitely not allowed and I spoke sharply to him, surprised. When I glanced in the rearview mirror, he had two paws on the window frame, straining against his seatbelt, and he barked sharply again. That was when I saw the box, seemingly of its own volition, roll slowly into the road.

Even though I was already practically at a stop, my foot hit the brake so hard that Cisco lost his balance, plopping all four paws back onto the bench seat, and my seat belt locked. Melanie plucked the ear buds out of her ears and stared at me. I slammed the car into Park and snatched the keys out of the ignition as I opened my door. "Stay here," I commanded her, and ran into the highway.

I could hear the yipping as soon as I opened the door. Cisco had obviously heard it long before. I scooped up the box with its moving, unwieldy contents about ten seconds before a truck driver blared his horn at me, but I was well back into my driveway when it swooshed past me with a rush of cold air and diesel fumes.

Melanie said, standing beside me, "What's that?"

"I told you to stay put," I snapped at her.

She followed me as I hurried back to the car. "What's in the box?"

"Puppies." My tone was short.

"Somebody mailed you puppies?" She scrunched up her face. "What do you need more dogs for?"

"They didn't mail them to me. Somebody dumped them off here. The puppies were abandoned. Get in the car and close the door. Hurry."

She did, and so did I. As soon as both doors were securely locked, I transferred the box to Melanie's lap and began to strip off the tape. "Hey!" she protested, but fell silent as I pulled back the cardboard and revealed what was inside.

Three fuzzy yellow pups about six weeks old squealed and wriggled and used each other as ladders as they tried to launch themselves to the top of the box and repeatedly tumbled down again. There were two males and a female, and though none of them looked to be in the kind of glowing health you might expect to see in purebred golden retriever puppies from a top breeder, the female was noticeably scrawnier than her sturdy brothers. I could see ribs, and her eyes were runny. She was shivering.

Melanie scrunched up her nose at the smell, which even I have to admit was not exactly potpourri, and said, "Eww. You're going to wash them, right?"

Cisco put both paws on the back of the front seat, panting with excitement as he strained to peer into the box. I quickly closed the lid of the box. "No," I said, "I'm taking them to the vet."

I fastened my seat belt and told Melanie to do the same. Cisco gave an indignant bark and lurched back into his own seat as I pulled out onto the highway.

Melanie lifted one flap of the lid. "The little one is cold," she observed.

I turned up the heat. "Take off your coat and put it over the box."

"This coat cost three hundred dollars!"

I glanced at her. "I got one just like it online for forty-five."

"Then take off your coat."

"I'm driving."

The pathetic mewling of the puppies would have melted the hardest heart, and after only another moment I heard her grumbling and wiggling out of her coat. She draped it over the box and I suppressed a smile.

"Is this the way to my dad's?" she asked when I reached an intersection and turned right.

"I told you, I'm taking the puppies to the vet. It won't take long. We'll call your dad from there."

I hadn't gone half a mile before I heard, over the whining and rustling from both the box and the backseat, the surprising sound of a familiar male voice. "What's up, pumpkin?"

"Daddy," Melanie said urgently, "I'm being kidnapped! I told her to take me home and she wouldn't do it!"

I glanced over at her quickly and saw Miles' face on the screen of her tablet. He said, "Let me talk to Raine."

She thrust the tablet at me and I swiped it away. "I'm driving!"

"I told you! She's kidnapping me!"

"Miles," I said loudly, "we're making a quick stop at the vet's. I'll bring her right over afterwards."

"Is everything okay?"

"Long story!" I had to shout now to be heard over the increasing cacophony, not to mention the fact that Melanie was deliberately trying to shield the device from me by hunching over it. "We're all fine!"

Miles said something I didn't hear, and eventually Melanie disconnected in a huff, flinging herself back against the seat and refusing to look at me, or at the box of puppies in her lap, for the remainder of the trip.

Cisco started to whine anxiously as soon as we turned into the gravel parking lot, and I couldn't blame him. He'd been injured in the line of duty not too long ago—the hair still hadn't completely grown back over his shoulder wound – and the vet's office was not one of his favorite memories. I told him as I put the car in Park, "It's okay, boy. You get to stay in the car this time. I'll bring you a cookie."

His ears perked up at that, and he stopped mid-whine.

Melanie started to fumble with the door handle, and I told her, "Stay there. I'll come around."

She scowled at me. "You're not going to leave me in the car, too, are you?"

I considered that for a moment. As a general rule, I am as responsible with my dogs as I would be with a child, so Melanie should have been as safe sitting in the car as Cisco was. The problem was that I trusted Cisco; I didn't trust Melanie. Also, I didn't think Miles would approve. So I said, "You can sit in the waiting room and play video games or something." I got out of the car and opened her door. "Hand me the box."

"My coat!" she protested, as I tucked the folds of her coat more securely around the puppies.

"We're two steps from the door," I told her impatiently. "Get over it."

She scrambled after me. "This is child abuse!"

I rolled my eyes.

I'm pretty well known around my vet's office, not only because of my own dogs, but because of the work I do with humane society and the golden retriever rescue group. Well, basically Maude and I *are* the local golden retriever rescue group, which is doubtless how a box of puppies landed beside my mailbox. Ethyl and Crystal, Doc's wife and daughter respectively, greeted me cheerfully from behind the front desk, and then oohed and ahhed over the contents of the box. Melanie, having snatched her coat off the box as soon as we got inside, stood in the center of the room glowering, and I pointed sternly to a chair. "Sit," I commanded.

In a moment she flung herself into the chair I'd indicated and powered up her iPad.

Ethyl she gave me a questioning look, and I responded with a shrug. "Babysitting," I said. I peered over the counter at Crystal, who was returning the last puppy to the box. "The little female doesn't look so great," I said. "I hate to walk in like this but I didn't want to take a chance."

"Not a problem," replied Crystal. "There are a couple of people ahead of you, but I'll take these little guys back and see if I can get them cleaned up a little. I'll call you when Dad is ready."

I crossed the room to sit beside Melanie, stopping to speak to Mrs. Dawson, whose bichon yapped noisily from his carrier, on the way. The bichon had been one of our grooming clients before we'd closed for remodeling, and I hoped would be again when we reopened. I asked after her dog's health, and she assured me he was just in for his shots. She asked when she could bring him in for a shampoo and trim, and I replied brightly, "Just give me a call after Christmas. We'll work him in." I was beginning to wonder if I would have to start washing dogs in my kitchen sink.

Mrs. Dawson lowered her voice confidentially and cut her eyes toward the back room, where Crystal had taken the puppies. "You know who those pups belong to, don't you?"

I had my suspicions, but I wanted to hear her say it.

"Lester Stokes' mama dog just had a litter a couple of months back. I was over there picking out a pumpkin with the kids and I thought I never would get them back in the car for playing with those puppies. He tried to make me take one home but they were too little to leave their mama, their eyes were barely open." She snorted. "Like I need another dog. This one is about all I can take care of as it is."

Crystal called her in just then, and I went to sit beside Melanie.

"My dad's last girlfriend had a house in Cocoa Beach," she said loudly. "I liked her a lot better."

I smiled weakly at the man sitting across from me, who returned a polite nod, and I picked up a six-month-old copy of *Dog Fancy*. Not only I had already read it, I had donated it to the waiting room. But I pretended to be absorbed, because it was better than having to make conversation with Melanie.

Crystal called me into the exam room twenty minutes later. I told Melanie to stay put and went inside. "Thanks for seeing me, Doc," I said. One of the puppies was on the steel examining table; the other two were in a wire crate in a corner. "Someone dumped them off this morning or late last night. I don't know how long they were out in the cold."

Doc Withers was a tall man with slightly stooped shoulders, steel-gray hair, and wire-rimmed glasses. The pawprint-patterned scrubs he wore did not detract from his dignity in the least; in fact they only enhanced it. He had been taking care of my dogs, Maude's dogs, and everyone else's dogs in the county for as long as I could remember, and there was no one else I would trust with my pets.

He held the squirming little pup up to face level and said, "Well, now, little fellow, you've had yourself quite an adventure, haven't you?" He glanced at me, bouncing the puppy experimentally in one hand. "Six pounds, three ounces."

Crystal put the puppy on a baby scale and reported, "Six pounds, three ounces."

I grinned. "How long has it been since you missed one, Doc?"

"Oh, it's got to be going on eight years now."

"Missed it by one ounce," Crystal said.

"Yeah, but that was before it peed all over the table."

We all laughed and while Doc examined the first two pups with easy efficiency, Crystal and I chatted about—what else?—dogs. Doc pronounced them to be golden/lab mixes, between six and seven weeks old, and in pretty good health, considering. He gave the two boys their shots and put them back in the great, but when he set the little female on the table, her legs splayed out from under her and she collapsed, too weak to stand, her chin banging the table top. Doc's face went grave, and Crystal and I were silent while he completed his examination.

"What do you think?" I asked quietly.

"Well, she's dehydrated," Doc said, "and running a little fever. I'd like to start her on antibiotics and I.V. fluids. We'll have to wait and see."

"Is she going to die?"

The voice that spoke at my side startled me, and I spoke more sharply than I had intended. "Melanie, I told you to wait outside."

Melanie shrugged, looked at the shivering little puppy cradled in Crystal's arms. Doc smiled at her. "We're going to try not to let that happen," he said.

I said unhappily, "It isn't—you don't think it could be parvo, do you?"

Parvovirus is an extremely dangerous, often fatal, and highly contagious disease in dogs that can live in the ground where an infected dog has been for up to a year. Most puppies have immunity from their mother's milk for the first eight weeks or so, and then they are inoculated. But sometimes, when the mother is not inoculated, there is no immunity to pass down.

Doc said, "That would be unusual this time of year. We see most of our Parvo in the spring."

"Could be canine flu," Melanie volunteered. "That's pretty bad."

I stared at her and she said, "I looked it up on the internet."

Doc said, "I'd like to keep the other two overnight just to see if they start showing symptoms, just in case. Why don't you check back with me tomorrow afternoon?"

I said, "Okay, thanks." I hesitated. "I don't suppose you have any idea where the puppies might have come from do you?"

"I have an idea," he said.

"Lester Stokes' bitch?" I suggested.

Melanie's eyes went wide behind her glasses. "My dad doesn't allow people to swear in front of me."

"It's not swearing when the word is used in its proper context," I told her impatiently. "A female dog is called a bitch. Look it up."

Doc tried to hide his amusement. "This is her second litter this year. Every puppy in the first one had demodex; people were bringing them in from all over the county."

"How old is she, anyway?"

"Eight or nine. Pretty little Golden. But too old to be bred that often."

I said, "Listen, if I can talk him into getting her spayed, would you give me a break on the surgery?"

Doc smiled. We had done this kind of thing before. "I'll do it for the cost of anesthesia. But good luck getting her in here. He makes money on those puppies when they're purebred."

"Thanks, Doc. I'll check with you tomorrow."

"Merry Christmas, Raine."

Lester Stokes had a little truck farm not three miles from the vet's office, and it would have been foolish not to stop by when I was this close—and also while I was still filled with enough righteous indignation to argue him down. So I grabbed a handful of dog biscuits from the jar by on the counter, bundled Melanie back into the car, and tossed Cisco his promised cookie as we took off for the Stokes' place. The rest of the dog biscuits I stuffed into my coat pocket, which did not make Cisco happy at all. He kept sniffing the air and stretching his head over toward the driver's side of the car, trying to see what I had done with them. You know that old joke: if you think your dog can't count, try putting three dog biscuits in your pocket and only giving him two. I see living proof of that every day.

"We're just going to make one quick stop," I told Melanie as I slowed the car and signaled a right turn at a battered rural mailbox.

Melanie said, "I don't understand why somebody would throw away a box of sick puppies."

I was surprised when I glanced at her and discovered she was not wired to her iPad. I sighed. "I don't either, honey."

The driveway wasn't very long, and it was lined on either side with the remnants of last year's garden: dried cornstalks, withered tomato plants, piles of rotting pumpkins. In the off-season Lester made his living doing odd jobs and selling firewood, and the approach to the small wood-frame house at the end of the drive was marred by a big pile of split firewood in the front yard. Beside it was a police car.

I couldn't hide my surprise as I pulled in behind the police car, and Cisco could not hide his excitement. He began to pant and paw the window as soon as he caught sight of the blue bubble light. I may have mentioned Buck Lawson is probably his favorite person in the world. "Stay here," I told Melanie. "Let me see what's going on."

The sound of a barking dog greeted me as I got out of the car, and I saw a white-faced golden retriever, her sagging teats evidence of a newly-weaned litter, lumber over to the gate of a small chain-link dog enclosure. Her barks were desultory and her tail wagged lowly and dispiritedly, and I was torn between rushing to comfort her and greeting the two people who stood beside the wood pile, one of them being my ex-husband. For once, I ignored my instincts—and the dog—and went over to Buck.

"Hey, Buck," I said.

He returned briefly, "Raine." He did not look happy to see me. "You mind holding on a minute while I talk to Nick?"

The person he referred to was a teenage boy in a sawdust-sprinkled sweatshirt and work gloves. There was a gas-powered log splitter beside him, and when I walked up he turned to load another log into it. "I already told you, I haven't seen Ashleigh in a week. I'm sorry about her old man, but everybody knows it was bound to happen sooner or later."

Nick. Ashleigh. Something stirred in the back of my brain, but an awful lot had happened in the past few days, and I couldn't put my finger on it.

Buck said, "Why do you think that?"

The boy shrugged without looking at Buck. "He was a mean drunk. He pissed off the wrong person this time." And there was a note of bitterness in his voice as he pulled the starter cord. The engine sputtered and died. "Somebody that could fight back."

I lifted an eyebrow at Buck, and Buck said, "Did he hit Ashleigh, Nick?"

He shrugged and pulled the starter cord again. "None of my business."

Buck said, "I thought you were her boyfriend."

Nick pulled the starter cord one more time, ignoring Buck, and suddenly I remembered where I had seen the girl in the photograph in Earl Lewis's kitchen before. She was the one who had been sobbing in the girl's bathroom at school yesterday when I went in to change. *You've got to come get me, Nick, something terrible has happened.*

I said, "Didn't you talk to her yesterday afternoon?"

Buck looked at me, and so did Nick.

I went on, "Didn't she call you after school and ask you to pick her up? She sounded pretty upset."

Nick straightened up, wiped his hands on his dusty jeans, and licked his lips. Buck waited silently.

"Look," Nick said, "we hung out a few times, that's all. She didn't have much else going on for her, and she was a good enough kid. So she called me to pick her up from school, but I told her I couldn't. That's it. I don't know where she is." He hesitated. "I hope she's okay."

"So do we," Buck said. "Look, Nick, four different people said they saw her leave her house late yesterday in a green car. It wasn't yours?"

He shook his head. "I don't have a car. Sometimes I borrow my dad's truck, but he was out delivering firewood yesterday."

Buck said, "Is that where he is now?"

"Yeah, we got two more loads to get out today. And he's going to be plenty mad if I don't get this one split by the time he gets back."

I said, "What about your brother? What kind of car does he drive?"

Again Buck glanced at me and Nick answered impatiently, "A Ford Explorer, red. And he's not even in town. His wife and he went to her folks in Michigan for Christmas. I told Ashleigh that."

Nick's brother, Keith, worked in the service department of the Ford dealership out on the highway, and his wife was a teller at the bank. I knew that because they had brought their six-month-old Golden to Dog Daze for training classes during the summer, and they had to take turns bringing him depending on who could get off work early. I admired them for their dedication.

"Some officers stopped by here last night about ten o'clock, looking to talk to you. No one was home."

"I went over to Mobley with some guys after the parade to see a movie."

"Oh yeah? What'd you see?"

"That new spaceship comedy. It was pretty good. The aliens were kind of hokey, though."

Buck smiled. "I'll have to check it out. Where were your folks?"

He shrugged. "My mom's doing double shifts at the Wal-Mart in Mobley from now till Christmas. Who knows where my dad was?"

He licked his lips again, looking uneasy. "Look, I've got to get this wood split. I'd help you if I could. I don't want anything bad to happen to Ashleigh."

Buck took a card from his pocket and handed it to Nick. "If you think of anybody she might have gone to stay with, or if you hear from her, you call me, okay?"

Nick took the card and glanced at it. "Yeah, okay, whatever. But–hey!"

I barely had time to glance around in the direction of his startled gaze before a golden blur came barreling by, almost knocked me off my feet with his speed and flung himself on Buck. "Cisco!" I cried, and lunged for his collar. Buck managed to catch Cisco's forepaws in mid-leap before they splattered his jacket with paw prints, and I commanded furiously, "Off!"

Cisco dropped to all fours, but only because Buck was rubbing his ears companionably. "Don't reward him for that," I snapped, and caught Cisco's collar. He was still wearing his seatbelt harness, and when I looked around, sure enough, the culprit who had freed him came sauntering up with her hands in her coat pockets.

"He wanted to get out," she explained matter-of-factly.

If Melanie had been one of my dogs, the look I gave her would have sent her slinking to her crate. She was, of course, oblivious.

"Cisco," I told her in a tone only slightly less sharp than the one had I used with Buck, "doesn't always have to get what he wants. I told you to stay in the car."

"Your phone was ringing."

Oh, great. I had completely forgotten to call Miles, and worse, I'd left the phone in the car so that he couldn't reach me. "It was probably your father. Go call him back and tell him we're on our way."

As usual, she ignored me, gazing at Buck with interest. "Are you a real cop?"

He smiled at her. "Yes, ma'am. Are you a real princess?"

She looked confused and wary. "I'm not a princess."

"Really? You sure look like one to me. And I'm a real cop."

That legendary charm of his even got Melanie to smile. She said, "Is this a crime scene? I've never been to a crime scene before."

"You still haven't," I told her. And to Buck, "This is Melanie, Miles's daughter. She's supposed to be waiting in the car." The last was added with a meaningful glare at Melanie, which she ignored. That seemed to amuse Buck.

"Pleased to meet you, Melanie," he said. "I'm Sheriff Buck Lawson."

In the background, the poor female Golden behind the chain link started to bark at Cisco, and he pricked up his ears in acknowledgement, reminding me why I had come here. I started to speak to Nick, but he was eyeing Cisco nervously. "Is that a drug dog?" he asked.

Odd. That was the second time in twenty-four hours I had been asked that question. I drew a breath to reply but Buck turned back to Nick and spoke over me smoothly.

"How come, Nick? You got drugs around here you're worried about?"

He frowned. "No. I just don't like strange dogs around, that's all."

"Oh, Cisco is a highly trained search dog," Buck assured him, and I couldn't help noticing he did not specify what Cisco was trained to search for. He reached down and patted Cisco's shoulder. Cisco grinned in agreement. "He's done a lot of work for the department."

As he spoke he slipped his hand under Cisco's collar, moving mine aside. His eyes met mine briefly, and I let go of Cisco, straightening up.

Nick said, "I don't think he can be here without a warrant. I think I studied that in civics class."

"What, the dog? He's just along for the ride. He's a good old dog, aren't you Cisco? You want to say hello to Nick?"

He released Cisco's collar and Nick shouted, "Hey!" as Cisco took off like a shot—just as I knew he would—for the kennel where the female Golden was caged.

I said, "Damn it, Buck!" and started after Cisco, but Buck put out his hand in a staying gesture. He was watching Nick carefully.

Melanie said, "I'm going to tell my dad about your language." But her eyes were bright with excitement.

"Is this a drug bust? Are you going to call the S.W.A.T. team? Wait until my mom hears about this!"

I muttered, "Oh Lord, just kill me now."

I knew what Buck was trying to do, but he had no right to use Cisco without my permission, and I wasn't about to lose to my dog just so he could make a teenage boy sweat over a couple of ounces of pot. Particularly when I was responsible for a minor child who already had enough dirt on me to make sure that she—and, in most likelihood, her father as well—was never alone with me again.

Nick said, "I'm going to call my dad."

"Sure," Buck agreed easily. "You do whatever you have to. And don't worry about the dog. I'll follow him around, make sure he doesn't get into anything."

"Oh, for heaven's sake!" I exploded under my breath, and I stalked off to reclaim my dog.

Cisco is in training. I remind myself of that every day. This is why, even though he regularly astonishes me on the tracking field, in the agility ring and yes, occasionally even with obedience exercises, I try never to make the mistake of expecting him to do what I ask every single time I ask it. My rule of thumb is that I never give a command until I'm ninety percent sure my dog will obey it. That's why I didn't try to call him away from his communion with the other golden retriever. Instead I chose to go and get him.

Usually when he saw me he would wag his tail and bound over to me. But whether it was the crisp winter air and his unexpected freedom in a strange place or he was just trying to show off for the other dog, as soon as I got within about ten feet of him he did a spin, a butt-tuck and took off like a mad thing across the yard. I stood stock still, fuming but trying not to show it, while he raced like a greyhound around the detached garage, across the back porch, over a flat-bed trailer, and into the barn. Melanie came up beside me.

"Doesn't look like much of a drug dog to me," she observed skeptically.

"Go back to the car," I told her, pronouncing each word carefully, "and get me a leash from the back. Right now."

She actually turned for the car, which gave me hope that Cisco might be as obedient.

I was halfway to the barn when Cisco came trotting out. He was carrying something the size of a child's toy in his mouth, and his tail was swishing with pride. I quickened my step and dug into my pocket for a dog biscuit. There were all sorts of things in a barn that dogs should never put in their mouths, and about a dozen of them were racing through my head at the moment. I commanded, "Cisco, here!" and made sure he saw the dog biscuit in my hand.

He pranced right to me, sat beautifully, and dropped the object at my feet. I gave him the dog biscuit, hooked his collar with one hand, and picked up the object he had dropped with the other.

"Well, well," Buck said behind me. "What have we here?"

I handed it over to him. It was a plastic baby Jesus, the kind that had been disappearing from Nativity scenes all over the county.

TEN

"Come on, Sheriff, it was just a prank." Nick's voice sounded a little desperate as he gazed into the box filled with purloined replicas of the Christ child that ranged from thumb-sized to the full-grown doll that had been stolen from the town Nativity only yesterday. Cisco, the famous drug dog, was now securely belted in the back seat of my car, but Melanie refused to be moved and was avidly taking in every word.

"It was Dave Harper; he's the one that dared me to do it. Said I couldn't get a hundred before Christmas, you know," Nick went on, almost pleading. "I didn't mean no harm. It was just a prank."

"Actually, it's theft by taking," said Buck, writing in his pad. "That's Dusty Harper's boy, over on Gap Creek?"

Nick nodded miserably. "Are you going to arrest me?"

"You and your daddy are going to have to come down to the office as soon as he gets back," Buck said. "You'll be charged, and you'll get a court date."

"He's gonna kill me," Nick said.

"Probably not. But I wouldn't be surprised if he took a strip out of your hide. I would if you were mine. What were you going to do with all of these things, anyway? "

Nick looked blank. Clearly he hadn't thought that far ahead.

Seeing the boy's wretchedness, Buck's face softened. "Look," he said, "I'm guessing there's probably under a thousand dollars' worth of merchandise here. That's petty theft, and that means no jail time if the judge is in a good mood. But you'd better make sure you're clean as a whistle before you go in front of the bench so if there's anything you're keeping to yourself, now would be the time to tell me."

Nick shifted his gaze away. I could see him chewing the inside of his cheek. Melanie, who had been watching the entire proceeding with great interest, piped up helpfully, "What about throwing those puppies away on the side of the road? That's a crime, isn't it?"

Nick stared at her, and Buck looked quizzically at me. "Someone dumped a box of golden-mix puppies at the end of my driveway," I explained. "And your dog just had a litter."

Nick scowled fiercely. "The old man said he was going to drown them. I thought I was doing a good thing. Now I guess I'm going to jail for that too."

I sighed. "No, they don't put you in jail for that." Though I privately thought they should. "But I would like to talk to your dad about it."

Buck said, "Looks like you're going to have to stand in line, Rainey."

Nick blurted, "Look, you came here asking about Ashleigh and I told you what I know. I can't do any more than that. I'm sorry about the puppies and I'm sorry about the stupid baby Jesuses but I can't go to jail, I just can't!" He looked up at Buck, eyes pleading. "Can't you help me out with my dad?"

Buck looked at me, and I looked at Buck, and we both were frowning. I gave a small jerk of my head and walked a little bit away. Buck came with me.

"I was at school yesterday with Cisco and I heard Ashleigh on the phone with Nick," I told Buck in a low tone. "I didn't put it together until now, but he's not telling the whole truth. She was practically hysterical on the phone. She said something terrible had happened and begged Nick to help her. Do you suppose she witnessed the murder?"

"Could be." Buck looked grim. "Or committed it."

I stared at him. "But—What about Camo Man?"

"Yeah, we tracked him down early this morning at home." A corner of his lips turned down dryly. "He'd been wilderness camping the past five days, snagged himself a five-pointer, dressed it out in the woods and took it to Leland Brown for processing. It all checks out. He claims some girl lost the ring when he gave her a ride to town yesterday afternoon."

"Ashleigh," I said, and he nodded.

"He picked her up at the Dairy Queen on Burdock Road last night and let her off at the town square. He saw her drop the ring and claims he tried to call her back, but she was in too much of a hurry to leave. So he picked it up and put it in his pocket. That must have been right before you saw him in the diner. The reason he was short on money was that he had just realized his wallet was missing."

"She stole his wallet?"

"That's the theory. He said she insisted on sitting in the back of the camper, and he thought she was just being cautious about getting in front with a strange man. Later he realized he'd left his jacket in the back with his wallet in it."

I felt a little defensive. "Well, he could be lying, you know."

"He could," agreed Buck. "But it doesn't seem likely. The members of his congregation speak very highly of him."

I smothered a groan. "He's a minister?"

"Bullard First Methodist. We found his wallet in one of the trashcans downtown. No cash."

I sighed. "So much for my detective instincts." Then I frowned. "Do you have a time of death yet?"

"It's looking like sometime between 11:00 Wednesday night, when the neighbors heard him peeling out of his driveway, and Thursday noon. Here's something else. Apparently he had a loud argument with one of his drinking buddies, Dusty Harper, Wednesday night, which would make Harper one of the last people to see him alive—besides Ashleigh, that is."

"Is that the same Harper--?"

Buck nodded. "The father of Dave Harper, Nick's partner in crime. We've pulled that kid in a few times for possession, and the apple didn't fall far from that tree if you know what I mean. There's a connection here, I just haven't figured it out yet. So I hope you don't mind me using Cisco to sweat Nick a little."

I shook my head absently. "Did you ever find the murder weapon?"

"No. We found the missing knife in the dishwasher, like you said, but it didn't match the knife wound."

"Her dad's been missing since Wednesday night," I murmured, "and it wasn't until after school on Friday that she decided to run away. I wonder why she waited so long." I murmured.

"Maybe she had some cleaning up to do."

I grimaced. "She didn't exactly finish, did she? She left all those bloody sheets in the bathtub. And she went to school like normal. It doesn't make sense to me."

"Murder and teenagers," Buck replied sagely, "rarely do. We'll put out an all-points on her. If she's in town, somebody knows where. If she's not, somebody saw her leave."

"I wonder how she got to the Dairy Queen. Burdock Road is nowhere near here, or her house, or her school."

"Whoever picked her up in the green car must've taken her. Your friend Camo Guy said she was still carrying the duffle bag."

"You need to find that green car," I said.

A corner of his lips turned down dryly. "We're on it, babe." He nodded his head, without turning, toward Nick. "Meanwhile, thanks for the tip. I figured the kid was holding something back, and now I have leverage. We still make a pretty good team, huh?"

I went all warm inside at that, and meeting the smile in his eyes was like coming home. We had always made a good team.

He glanced over his shoulder to where Melanie was sorting through the box of evidence—the Nativity figurines—with the absorption of a forensics technician. Good thing Buck wasn't planning to dust for fingerprints. "So how long are you babysitting? Are you going to make it to the Department party tonight?"

I was a little taken aback. The Sheriff's Department Christmas Party was something of a family tradition, and I had been worrying about whether or not to attend for weeks now. My little voice told me the best thing to do would be to bow out gracefully, but earlier in the year, when it actually looked as though Buck and I might be getting back together, I had picked up this absolutely gorgeous little red dress on sale at the mall that would be perfect for the party. It seemed a shame to waste it, and where else would I get a chance to wear it around here?

When Buck and I had been broken up before I had always gone as Uncle Roe's guest, but now that he was no longer sheriff my claim to a seat at the table wasn't quite as clear. He and Aunt Mart were planning to go, of course, and I knew they probably expected me to join them, but the whole thing seemed a little awkward to me. On the other hand, that dress made me look like a size two, which I wasn't, and how often did that happen?

I shrugged uncomfortably. "Oh, I don't know. I really don't belong there."

He grinned. "Give me a break. You and Cisco have solved enough crimes this year alone to qualify for your honorary junior detective badge—including the case of the missing baby Jesuses just today. Besides, it's going to be kind of a tribute to Roe this year, since we didn't get to give him a retirement party. Some of the guys are doing a skit and everything. He'll be disappointed if you're not there."

I smiled reluctantly. "Well, I would miss that cherry ham you boys order every year. Maybe I'll try to make it down."

"Good for you." He turned and started back to Nick and Melanie. "Whatcha doing there, princess?"

Melanie examined a figurine, frowned a little, and put it back in the box. "I saw a movie once where the bad guys used these Virgin Mary statues to hide drugs."

Buck looked impressed. "Any luck?"

"Nah. I think these yokels are too dumb to figure out how to do that."

Nick glared at her and Buck suppressed a chuckle. "I wouldn't doubt you're right. However..." He turned to Nick and held out his hand. "You can turn over that joint you've got in your pocket now and save yourself a lot of grief later."

So *that* was why Nick had been so worried about drug dogs. I watched appreciatively as Nick, looking utterly dejected, fumbled in his jeans pocket and drew out a half-smoked marijuana cigarette. Melanie's jaw dropped in amazement and delight, and Buck winked at her. "That's why they pay me the big money, princess."

Lester Stokes arrived a few minutes later, and I hurried Melanie to the car before she heard some language worth reporting to her father. My phone started ringing as I was fastening my seat belt. I snatched it up.

"Miles, I am so sorry—"

"Is Melanie okay?" he demanded.

"Yes, she's right here—"

"Are you okay?"

"Yes, of course, I just—"

"Meet me at your house," he said, and disconnected. He did not sound happy.

He wasn't. He was leaning against the driver's door of his black Lexus when I drove up, his arms folded across his chest, his face tight. Melanie grabbed her iPad and had her door open almost before the car stopped.

"Hey, Dad, guess what?" she cried, running up to him. "We rescued puppies from the highway! Then we went on a drug bust and interrogated witnesses and examined evidence!"

She was as animated as I had ever seen her, and I thought that might have earned me a few points with her father. But no. He spared a smile for her and ruffled her hair as he said, "Oh, yeah? You can tell me all about it on the way to Far Heights. We're going to have lunch at the lodge and then hit the slopes, how does that sound?"

"Cool!" She climbed in the car and added just before she slammed the door, "And I met Sheriff Buck!"

That did nothing to improve Miles's disposition, and I approached him cautiously. "Miles, I'm sorry we're late. We had a few stops, and I would have called but—"

"But clearly you don't know how to dial a phone, any more than you know how to answer one."

"Hey, that's not fair." I bristled. "You could have called Melanie. And I told her to call you, more than once."

His eyes were cold. "I trusted you with my daughter," he said, "and you showed her less respect than I show your damn dogs. Don't ever do anything like this again." He got inside the car and slammed the door.

I was so astonished that he had started the engine and was backing up before I could think to shout, "Watch your language! She'll turn you in!"

Not my finest moment. And he drove away without even looking back.

I got Cisco out of the car and trudged up the front steps, feeling about as Scrooge-like as I had ever felt this close to Christmas. I opened the door and stopped dead in my tracks, staring in astonishment. Cisco came to a halt beside me. I'd like to think it was because he was that well trained, or because he was as amazed as I was. In fact it was because neither one of us could have taken a step forward without becoming entangled in an elaborate spider web of glittering Christmas ribbon.

It stretched from the staircase to the mantel to the coat rack to the end table, around the sofa and over the easy chair, through the rails of the banister and around a floor lamp. It encircled a dog crate twice, wrapped around the draperies, looped over another table, and made a beeline for the kitchen. My entire house had been wrapped up like one great big Christmas present.

I gingerly lifted a length of the ribbon and ducked under, then stepped over, and urged Cisco to do the same. Feeling a little like Tom Cruise breaking into a museum, weaving my way in and out of the network of criss-crossing lines, I made my way to the kitchen with Cisco at my side. I wished I had had a camera. The video would have gone viral on YouTube.

Crouched under the kitchen table with her head on her paws—and a length of ribbon twisted around one of them—gazing at me with an expression that was part sheepish and part proud, was Mischief. This is why I have dogs. I stood there, hands planted on hips, and I burst into laughter. My mood wasn't nearly as foul as it had been when I walked in. Sometimes the Christmas spirit sneaks in on four paws.

I freed Mischief from the ribbon tangled around her paw and she scampered off to find her sister, who was, of course, obediently waiting in her crate where she belonged. Yes, I know. The average person would wonder why I didn't find some kind of lock for Mischief's crate that she couldn't master or why I even bothered to put her in her crate at all. I asked myself the same thing now and then, but the truth is, she had me pretty well trained. I was starting to enjoy her exploits as much as she was.

I went through the house unwinding the ribbon from various objects and had almost reached the living room when Maude arrived, followed closely by Sonny. I had forgotten that they had promised to help me with the Christmas mailing for Golden Rescue today. They stood at the door for a moment, taking it all in, and then Maude observed in her dry British way, "Interesting choice."

Sonny had brought her service dog, Hero, and all three of my dogs scampered to greet him, entangling themselves in ribbon along the way. There was the usual confusion of sorting dogs and people, which was made even more complicated by the fact that Maude had brought a casserole and Sonny had brought cookies. In fairly short order I rescued the food, turned the dogs out into the play yard, and explained about Mischief's sudden interest in holiday decorating while the three of us finished clearing out the ribbon jungle.

"Yesterday I came home and she had taken out all the silver Christmas balls and lined them up across the floor," I said. "She even managed to put one in Magic's crate."

"Clearly, she thinks the place could use some sprucing up," Maude said, and Sonny was chuckling out loud.

"I think she just likes leading you on a treasure hunt," Sonny said.

"Yeah, well, you know what they say," I responded. "One dog's treasure is another girl's trash." And to prove it, I wadded up the last of the ribbon, stuffed it in the trash and headed toward the kitchen. "Come on, let's eat. I've had a pretty full morning—a pretty full twenty-four hours, as a matter of fact."

"So I see." Maude, following me into the kitchen, picked up a high-heeled, leopard- print shoe from the center of the table and examined it with a lifted eyebrow. Sonny found the mate protruding from the half-open bread box.

For a moment I drew a blank, and then I exclaimed, "Oh, no! Those shoes danced with President Kennedy! Tell me she didn't chew them!" I snatched the shoe from Maude and examined it quickly. "How did she even find them?"

Sonny handed me the other shoe. "I assume we're still talking about Mischief?"

"Who else?" Both shoes appeared to be unharmed, and I looked around for the box.

"She says she's innocent," Sonny said.

"Yeah, well, all evidence to the contrary."

"She says it's not evidence. It's magic."

I spared Sonny a look that clearly said, *Enough, already,* and she shrugged good-naturedly. "I can only tell you what I know," she said.

"Might one ask how your dog came to almost chew up a pair of shoes that danced with a former president?"

That was from Maude, and I gave up looking for the box and explained about Miss Esther and her eccentric gift while I warmed the casserole in the microwave and set the table. "She's a sweet old thing," I said, "but I'm afraid she thinks the shoes are more valuable than they are. She says the government has been after them for years."

Sonny examined the shoes skeptically. "They're vintage," she admitted, "but I don't think even a museum would want a pair of shoes that may or may not have danced with a president. Do you suppose she really knew John Kennedy?"

I shrugged. "She knew a lot of famous people."

"A pity the shoes don't fit you," Maude said. "This being the season for parties and all."

That reminded me of the Sheriff's Department Christmas party tonight, and that reminded me of my morning with Buck and the missing Ashleigh. I filled them in on the events of the past twenty-four hours— including my unexpected overnight guests and the even more unexpected box of puppies—while we ate.

"What I'm still unclear on," Maude said with a meaningful look at me, "is how you lost control of Cisco in the first place."

Maude doesn't mean to be judgmental; she is quite simply a perfectionist dog trainer. And since she taught me everything she knows, she expects me to be the same. Which I am. More or less.

"Well, it certainly wasn't my idea." I couldn't help being a little defensive. "Cisco has always been an idiot about Buck, and Buck reinforces it. Cisco just can't be trusted around him."

"It seems to me a little training in impulse control might be appropriate."

"Tell that to Cisco." But I privately thought Maude was right, and I felt guilty for not being a better trainer. We spent a good deal of time working around law enforcement, and Cisco's enthusiasm around Buck was not only embarrassing, it might one day very easily prove dangerous.

"He runs to Buck because Buck gives him undivided attention," Sonny commented. "That's all he wants."

"That's what everybody wants," I muttered.

"He's out of control because he doesn't have a job," was Maude's opinion. "He's a working dog and he needs something to do. Since the kennel closed down you've stopped training agility, and how long since he went to tracking class?"

"Come on, I missed one month." The thing about tracking class is that it is invariably held at sunup, regardless of rain, snow, ice or sleet, and there is usually an hour's drive involved to get to the open field or wooded hill where the course has been set. Who can blame a person for wanting to sleep in now and then? "And I can hardly train agility when my equipment's in storage."

Maude gave me a stern look, which I avoided. Many of the top competitors, I knew, trained with nothing but a set of portable jumps and weave poles. In the snow.

"Cisco says he's a star," Sonny insisted. "He feels his talents are being under-utilized. When he runs away, he's just looking for a way to be useful."

Maude lifted an eyebrow. "For once you and I are in agreement, my dear."

Even I couldn't argue with that. He had certainly proven himself useful when he had discovered Nick's cache of stolen treasure...even though I had yet to be convinced that had not been an accident.

"Speaking of runaways," Sonny said, "if it wasn't her boyfriend who was driving the car Ashleigh was seen getting into, who do the police suppose it was?"

"No theories yet." I was glad to turn the conversation to something other than my failures as a dog trainer. "She was carrying a bag, though, so she must have planned to be gone for a while. What I can't figure out is how she ended up way out on Burdock Road, and then why she'd turn around andhitch another ride into town."

"Strange," said Sonny. "The police don't really think she killed her own father, do they? A fourteen-year-old?"

"One certainly hears worse on the news these days," Maude observed. "Personally, however, I wouldn't trust the word of a boy who would toss a box of puppies out of a car. He's got her stashed away somewhere, you mark me."

"Come on, Maude, he *did* bring them to Rescue," I said. I was talking about the puppies now. "And I'm sure he didn't really toss them out. He just left them by my mailbox."

"As though we have nothing else to do with our lives but take care of the mistakes of every irresponsible breeder in the county," returned Maude, who had never turned down a homeless Golden in her life. "And unlimited funds, of course."

"If the female does have parvo," I said unhappily, "it will cost a fortune to bring her through it."

"Well, that's why we're here, isn't it?" Sonny started to rise to clear the table, but I saw her wince and waved her to stay seated. She had arrived with her cane today, and I had not seen her do that in several months.

"Sorry," she said as Maude and I took the dishes to the sink. "The cold weather is starting to work its dark magic my bones. I can't wait to get to the coast. My sister says it's seventy degrees today."

Sonny had a degenerative rheumatic condition that had reduced her to a wheelchair when I first met her; after she had adopted Mystery—and then Hero—I had seen a marked improvement, but I knew there were days, and always would be, when she could not get out of bed. I was glad she was getting out of the mountains for the winter and felt guilty for begrudging her, however briefly, the escape.

Maude said, "As a matter of fact, I've the chance to get away to a warmer climate this Christmas, too, and I think I'll take it, by George." She started rinsing the plates and placing them in the dishwasher. "You recall my sister's boy who moved to Florida a few years back and opened that hotel? He's getting married over the holidays and he's bringing the whole family over for the occasion. It will be quite a treat for me—I haven't seen some of them in forty years."

Sonny congratulated her happily and shared her excitement, but I just stared. Maude *never* took vacations—not real ones, anyway. Dog shows, seminars and conferences hardly counted since I was usually with her, and we had spent every Christmas together since I was a child. I said, "But—this is awfully sudden, isn't it? I mean, you didn't say anything. And what about the dogs?"

"Well, I couldn't make any plans until I knew whether or not we'd be open over the holidays, now could I? And of course I wouldn't consider going if the hotel weren't dog friendly. Which it is. "

I quickly mustered a smile. "It sounds great. Lucky you."

"Just so," agreed Maude with a crisp and pleased nod of her head. "Now let's see if we can raise a few funds, shall we? Spaying that Golden bitch of Lester Stokes is not going to be free, either—and that's assuming he agrees to it."

"I'll go back out there in a few days," I promised. "He wasn't about to agree to anything today."

I let the dogs in and got them settled in their places—Hero under Sonny's chair, Cisco beside mine, and the two girls watching us hopefully from the braided rug by the door. There is an unwritten rule among dogs: no one willingly leaves the kitchen while people are sitting at the table. There was, after all, a plate of homemade butterscotch cookies in the center of it, and as every patient dog knows, accidents do happen.

Years ago we had started sending out Christmas cards to all our clients at Dog Daze Boarding and Training, whether they had been in once for a quick nail trim or taken a year's worth of training lessons from us. We had built up quite a mailing list, and the solicitation letters for Golden Rescue we included in each card usually netted us a few hundred dollars each year. With the economy the way it was, I did not expect to net much above the cost of the mailing this year, but we had to keep trying. Besides, it was important to remind people that Dog Daze would be reopening soon.

I hoped.

Shortly after Thanksgiving, Maude, Sonny and I had gathered all our dogs, posed them in Santa hats, and spent the day photographing them until we finally got one in which all the dogs were looking more or less at the camera and their hats were on more or less straight. A few hours with Photoshop and we had a Christmas card no soft-hearted animal lover could resist. All we had to do was tuck the letter from Rescue inside each card and affix a mailing label and stamp. The work went fairly quickly, but I was glad to have to help. I munched cookies while I stuffed envelopes, and I casually mentioned my plans to go to the Sheriff's Department Christmas party that night.

Maude seemed surprised. "Really? I didn't think you'd go this year."

I shrugged. "I hadn't planned on it, but Buck made a point of inviting me. They're doing something special for Uncle Roe."

Sonny said, "I thought you said Miles is in town."

"He is. Or was." I couldn't help frowning a little as I stuffed another plea for money into a Christmas card. "Not that it matters. Or would have mattered, even if he wasn't mad at me."

"Mad at you?" Sonny arched an eyebrow. "What could you possibly done to have made him mad? Aside from badgering him with environmental petitions and putting your name on every lawsuit that's been filed against him in this county, of course."

Since she was the attorney of record for all of those lawsuits and the environmental petitions, she hardly had room to talk, and she knew it. "Miles doesn't care about that stuff. We agreed to disagree a long time ago." And I shrugged, pretending a nonchalance I was very, very far from feeling. "But you're probably right. He was interesting enough, but there was never any chance of it going anywhere. It was a disaster waiting to happen."

Maude and Sonny exchanged a look I didn't like or understand.

"He always seemed a pleasant enough chap to me," Maude said, making crisp, efficient folds in the stack of solicitation letters at her elbow before passing them to Sonny to be inserted into the cards. "And you did seem to enjoy his company."

Despite her reserved British manner, Maude was not above fishing for information, and I suppose she was entitled. She had seen me through too many heartbreaks not to have something of an investment in my personal life.

"I barely know him," I said. "We don't have anything in common. And..." I frowned again. "He called my guys 'dogs.' Damn dogs, to be precise."

"The villain," observed Maude mildly. "He should be flogged."

Sonny was trying not to smile. "Well, I can certainly see how that would put him on your *persona non gratis* list, but it doesn't explain what you did to get on his."

"It was a stupid misunderstanding. He didn't think I was being responsible with Melanie. She wasn't out of my sight for one minute, and most of the time we were with a police officer, for heaven's sake. How much more responsible can you get? He just doesn't understand how things work around here. He was completely unreasonable."

They both were tactfully silent, and after a moment, a corner of my lips turned down in dry acknowledgement. "Okay," I admitted. "So he had a point. But it doesn't matter." I was trying hard to make myself believe that. "Like I said, it was fun hanging out with a rich guy, but it never would have gone anywhere. He's not my type."

Maude's brows shot up into her steel-gray bangs. "Now, I simply can't let that pass. My dear, you can't be unaware that this new fellow of yours is exactly like the old one? Be that for good or ill I can't say, but he is *definitely* your type."

I stared at her. "What are you talking about?"

Sonny shook her head, looking amused. "Think about it, Raine. Good-looking, powerful, charming, in a position of authority…"

"Mild-tempered, easygoing, well-liked," added Maude.

Sonny finished, "Who are we describing?"

I still didn't get it, and Sonny laughed softly. "Miles is just another version of Buck, only without the uniform. I can't believe you didn't realize that. I thought that was why you were attracted to him in the first place."

I scowled fiercely. "I never said I was attracted to him. Besides, that's ridiculous. They're nothing alike."

Sonny and Maude looked at each other again, but neither said a word. I slapped another stamp on an envelope. "Besides," I said, "even if they were…"

I stopped, staring at the envelope on the table before me.

"Guess who lives on Burdock Road?" I said, and slowly raised my eyes to them in triumph. "Keith and Emmy Stokes—Nick's brother! I think I know where Ashleigh is!"

ELEVEN

There is nothing, and I mean *nothing*, as much fun as walking into a party looking hot and feeling like a hero. Well, okay, I've heard tell that a clean run in an agility trial is even better, but since I've never had one I can't testify to that.

My red dress had a square neck that showed enough cleavage to make me feel just a little naughty—but not enough to scandalize my aunt—and a flirty skirt that flared well above the knee and made my legs look a mile long. My silver shoes had three-inch heels and big, red sequined buckles on the toes. My hair, which had grown out over the past few months, curled perfectly around my collarbone. I spent a long time primping and preening in front of the mirror, because in my line of work there aren't a lot of opportunities to look gorgeous. I appreciate them when they come.

The Sherriff's Department's annual Christmas Party was held in the Legion Hall, as were most holiday parties with more than ten guests that weren't church-affiliated. The employees pitched in to have a ham dinner with all the fixings catered, and traditionally the sheriff supplied the beer and wine. I could see by the number of happy people with glasses in their hands that Buck had kept up the tradition.

There was a big, fragrant Christmas tree in one corner and a woodsy-smelling fire going in the fireplace. The buffet table was covered with a white cloth and scattered with colorful glass Christmas balls. Covered aluminum chafing trays added the aromas of butane and good food to the mix.   Mannheim Steamroller was on the stereo and the wood-floored building echoed with laughter. I left my coat in the foyer, fluffed up my hair, and felt like a million bucks when I walked in.

Of course I knew everyone there. A couple of the wives—who had naturally been on my side in the divorce—hugged me and told me how great it was to see me.   Even Deke, apparently moved by the Christmas spirit and at least one beer, nodded pleasantly at me and commented, "Looking sharp, Ms.—uh…" He never had gotten used to not calling me by my married name.   "Raine," he finished awkwardly. In the spirit of the season, I smiled and thanked him.

My aunt, looking sharp herself in a beaded black sheath and smelling of Sand & Sable perfume,

Donna Ball

embraced me, and Uncle Roe kissed my cheek. "There she is, the girl of the hour," he declared. "Why in the world you just don't go ahead and join the force, I'll never know."

I laughed. "If things don't pick up in the dog-training business, I just might have to do that."

Across the room, Buck lifted his mug to me and smiled, and I felt a warm glow spread all the way out to my fingertips. He looked particularly handsome in a tan wool sweater and the suede sports coat I'd given him the last Christmas we were married. It was oddly pleasant to see him out of uniform, relaxed and happy and surrounded by his peers, drinking a beer. He glanced a question toward his mug, and I lifted my index finger. He turned to get me a beer.

"Honestly, Raine, I'd think you'd have enough to do this time of year without running all over the county helping these boys solve their cases," said Aunt Mart. "Heaven knows I do."

"Actually," I said, "I wouldn't have figured it out at all if it hadn't been for the puppies. That's how I ended up at Lester Stokes' place this afternoon, and that's how I met Nick."

"What puppies?" my aunt asked.

So I told her about the box of puppies that Nick had left by my mailbox, and how I had gone out there to talk to his father about retiring their breeding program at the same time Buck had been trying to question him about Ashleigh. "I knew he was trying to hide something," I said, "I just couldn't figure out what."

"Of course he had a lot to hide," Buck said, coming up beside me. "Petty theft, misdemeanor possession…"

I nodded and accepted the beer he had brought me. In honor of the holidays, beer was served in glass mugs instead of in the can, and it was amazing how much better it tasted that way.

"When he mentioned his brother," I went on, "I remembered we had trained his Golden—from one of Lester's litters, naturally—over the summer. Then when I saw his address on Burdock Road—about two blocks from the Dairy Queen—it just made sense that Nick would try to help his girlfriend out by letting her stay in his brother's empty house while they were away."

"And it all made a lot more sense," Buck added, "when you remembered that when the wife brought the dog to training classes, she was driving a green Chevy. They left the keys to the Chevy with Nick's folks while they were on vacation."

"The poor child," Aunt Mart said. "She didn't even know her daddy was dead."

"Oh, she knew, all right." Buck's tone was a little grim. "It's been all over the radio, and besides, Nick had to have told her. What we don't know yet is why she continued to hide out there when she knew we were looking for her, and why she ran away in the first place."

Buck had called me to let me know Ashleigh had been found at Keith Stokes' house, and that they had brought her in for questioning. I hadn't heard anything else, and I was anxious for the details.

"So what did she say?" I asked. "Do you still think she was involved in her father's death?"

My aunt's eyes went wide and Buck shook his head. "Luckily for her, the medical examiner's report came back today, the wound was inflicted by a person about the same height as the victim. There's no way a five-foot-tall girl could have done it."

"So what was she doing in town Friday afternoon?" That was the one thing that had been puzzling me all day. "She had a safe hideout, and then she blew it by hitching a ride into town."

"Who knows? She wasn't making much sense when I left. She claimed she didn't know anything about the bloody sheets in the tub, and the last time she saw her father was when he stormed out of the house drunk Wednesday night. There are rules about interrogating minors, and until she's officially declared a ward of the court she can't be assigned counsel."

"You didn't take that poor child to jail?" Aunt Mart sounded alarmed.

"Yes, ma'am," Buck admitted, and he added quickly, "but we released her to social services as soon as they got there. The only thing we had on her was petty theft, and when we called the minister and told him we had her, he decided not to press charges. He said the kid had enough problems as it was, and he's probably right. She'll probably go into foster care until the court makes a decision."

"Well, I should think you could show a little more compassion for the victim, it being Christmas and all."

Buck drew a breath to reply but Uncle Roe said, "Now, Martie, let the man do his job." Then to Buck, "If you ask me it's that boy, Nick, you ought to be looking into, and that Harper kid. There's a bad card if I ever saw one."

Buck said, "We added obstruction to the charges against Nick, which will probably keep him in jail overnight, but he'll bond out by morning. I still think he knows more about Earl Lewis than he's letting on, and the girl is definitely keeping something back. She had eyes like a scared rabbit. I'll tell you what's bothering me, though. In three out of four of the burglaries we investigated, neighbors reported seeing a red pickup truck. Dusty Harper drives a red pickup truck and he lives in the same trailer park as Lewis did. His kid, Dave, is best buddies with Nick, and he even admitted he was the one who dared Nick to steal those baby Jesuses. But not a scrap of real evidence to tie either one of them to Lewis. How does that happen? "

Aunt Mart rolled her eyes and slipped her arm through mine. "These men never stop talking shop, do they? Even at a party! Let's get a table. These shoes are killing me. Yours are awful pretty."

To be honest, I would have rather talked shop with the men than shoes with my aunt, but it was a party, after all. We chose a table where a couple of members of the administrative staff had settled and made small talk with them for a while. Then Aunt Mart turned to me, her eyes sparkling, and said, "Now for the big news. Roe gave me my Christmas present early this year and you'll never guess."

"Diamonds?" I suggested. "Emeralds?"

She laughed and pressed her hands together. "We're going on a cruise! Can you believe that? Twenty years and I haven't been able to get that man out of the state, and now he wants to take me to Antigua!"

"Aunt Mart, that's wonderful." I was delighted for her. "You're going to have so much fun! When are you leaving?"

"Christmas Eve," she said, and suddenly I wasn't so delighted. If my expression fell she didn't notice, because she rushed on, "You don't mind taking Majesty, do you? It's only two weeks. We'll be back right after New Year's."

"Mind? Are you kidding? I've already hung her stocking!" I found a smile. Having Majesty back was the silver lining in a rather dark cloud, of course, but...Christmas. We always had Christmas dinner together.

"Do you know I had to get out a map to even find out where Antigua *was*?"

Annabelle, the night dispatcher, leaned across the table and said, "It's in South America, isn't it? My brother-in-law, J.T., was there last spring and he said..."

I smiled absently and sipped my beer and let my eyes roam around the room until I saw Buck and Uncle Roe coming toward us, still deep in conversation. There's a saying that old cops, like old soldiers, never die; they simply fade away. But in the case of Uncle Roe, it was clear he would neither die *nor* fade away, but continue to uphold law and order in Hanover County as long as there was a county to uphold law and order in. Over the past couple of months he had been working with the sheriffs in the surrounding three mountain counties to form a cold case squad from retired officers and other volunteers, so he no longer went to office every day. But nothing went on in this county he didn't know about, and he wasn't hesitant about offering his assistance to the department whenever he thought it was needed.

As you might imagine, Buck had mixed feelings about that. On the one hand, he had gone to work for Uncle Roe since before the ink was even dry on his criminal justice degree, and like just about everyone else in the county, he worshipped the ground my uncle walked on. On the other hand, Buck was sheriff now, and it couldn't be easy, trying to find your own place in the shadow of a legend.

"What did he say when you questioned him?" Roe was saying as they reached the table.

"What could he say? We had witnesses." Buck's eyes were roaming the room, the way they did when he was looking for a way to change the subject.

"Who's that?" I asked, sipping my beer.

Uncle Roe sat beside me. "That fellow we were talking about, Harper. He was one of the last people to see Lewis alive."

"But he *was* alive," Buck pointed out, still standing. "The neighbors corroborate the daughter's story that they had a fight in the front yard on Wednesday night, then Dusty drove away."

"Anybody know what it was about?"

Buck shook his head. "Dusty says Lewis owed him money. He seemed pretty pissed that he wouldn't get to collect, with Lewis being dead and all."

"Fine fellow," observed Uncle Roe.

Aunt Mart leaned across me to admonish, "If you two don't hush with that talk about work I'm never coming to one of these parties again." She said that every year. "Buck, sit down, for Heaven's sake. You look like you're waiting for a bus."

Buck grinned and took the chair beside Uncle Roe. "Well, maybe for a minute. They ought to be opening up the chow line pretty soon."

"Oh, wait," Aunt Mart exclaimed, "I've got to get a picture." She dug in her purse for her camera. "Annabelle, honey do you mind? You just push that big button. Raine, switch places with Roe. How's my lipstick? Now won't this be pretty with the tree in the background?"

We spent a few moments changing places, shuffling chairs and checking lipstick. The flash clicked the perfect shot as we leaned in close, and at Annabelle's insistence, said, "Reindeer!" I found myself sitting next to Buck, while Uncle Roe rested his arm across the back of my aunt's chair, their heads close together. Annabelle took a couple of more shots and handed the camera back over to Aunt Mart.

"I'll e-mail these to you, Raine," Aunt Mart said, checking the pictures in the digital display. "And the ones from the parade last night, too. Oh, look here's Majesty. Doesn't she look sweet?"

I leaned over to see the picture but the glare on the screen made it difficult. "Send it to me," I said. "Maybe I'll use her in next year's Christmas card."

Aunt Mart put the camera away. "Did you find out anything about that poor little baby?" she asked. "Who would do such a thing?"

Buck shook his head. "Unless the mother comes forward, or some witness does, it's not likely we'll ever find out who left her there. With all the people in from out of town this time of year, it could have been anyone."

Aunt Mart's frown was troubled. "Well, I suppose it makes me feel better to think it was some stranger. I'd hate to find out it was somebody from around here who was that desperate and no one knew it." Aunt Mart was very active in the local charities, and when someone in need went without help, she took it personally.

Clarisse, who was sitting beside Annabelle, hadn't heard about the abandoned infant and wanted to know the details. Aunt Mart was happy to fill them in, and Uncle Roe was reminded of a similar incident that had happened twenty years earlier. While they chatted, Buck and I sat in easy silence for a while, gazing around the room, waving at people we knew.

Buck smiled at me. "You look pretty tonight, Raine. I like your hair."

I felt a little flush. I admit it. "Thanks. It's fun to get dressed up."

He sipped his beer, and we enjoyed a moment of feeling comfortable together. There had not been very many of those lately. "Have you got your tree yet?"

I shook my head. "Not yet. Maybe this weekend." Usually he and Uncle Roe would go out and cut two trees, one for me and one for Aunt Mart, then deliver and set them up around the middle of the month. After Uncle Roe's heart attack I certainly didn't expect him to be tramping all over the mountain looking for Christmas trees, and I wasn't about to ask Buck. Everything was different this year.

I added, "Mischief has been busy decorating, though." And he laughed along with everyone else as I told the stories of Mischief's exploits. For a moment it was just like old times.

And then Buck saw someone at the door and his eyes lit up with a smile. He excused himself and stood. "Y'all enjoy the party," he said. He touched my shoulder lightly. "See you later."

I craned my neck around to watch him cross the room to greet the new arrival. Wyn was stunning in a blue, scoop-neck, stretch velour tunic and silver leggings, with her dark hair drawn over one shoulder in a silver clasp. Her eyes lit up when she saw Buck, too, and she stretched out her hands. I turned away when he leaned in to hug her.

I don't know why I hadn't expected her to be here. But I hadn't. And there was a moment when it was actually hard to catch my breath.

My table had gone stone silent, and everyone was looking at me, breaths suspended, waiting. But whatever they were waiting for, they weren't going to get it from me. I was determined to be mature about this thing. I turned to Uncle Roe with a smile and elbowed him playfully in the ribs. "So, you! A cruise, huh?"

Everyone relaxed and started to enjoy themselves again, and I pretended to as well. But the thing about being mature is that it hurts like hell.

It was a good party. Really. I laughed along with everybody else when four of the deputies got up dressed in Santa hats and did a tribute in song to Uncle Roe with customized lyrics to the tune of "The Twelve Days of Christmas". I applauded along with everyone else as Buck gave a report on the collections the department had made for the Toys for

Underprivileged Children drive, and when he handed out the year-end awards and commendations to officers who had distinguished themselves. And when he called Uncle Roe up to the front and presented him with a framed "Lifetime Achievement of Service" award, along with a gold-plated commemorative department badge, I was misty-eyed. I was glad I hadn't missed it.

I'm sure the ham and mashed potatoes and green bean casserole were delicious; I don't remember tasting them, but they usually are. Wyn came up to me in the buffet line and said an uncertain, "Hi, Raine." I said hi back because we used to be friends, but there wasn't much to say after that. It was nice of her to make the effort, though.

And every time I saw Buck touch her back the way he used to touch mine or lean in to say something to her and then laugh or even just rest his arm across her chair and absently toy with her hair...well, it was like somebody punched a hole in my stomach and pulled out my guts. I was furious with him for inviting her, but then why shouldn't he? She was a former member of the department much as Uncle Roe was; everyone was glad to see her and everyone knew she and Buck were together now. All things considered, she had more right to be here than I did, and she probably should have been mad at *me*. But knowing that did not stop the icicle that stabbed through my chest when she found herself standing under the mistletoe and Buck kissed her on the lips, and it wasn't exactly a quick peck either. Even the most mature person would have trouble dealing with that.

As the hour grew later and the crowd grew noisier, Uncle Roe was pressed into service handing out the Secret Santa gag gifts everyone exchanged each year. I was convinced my face would crack if I gave one more phony laugh, so I thought that might be a good time to sneak out. I hugged my aunt, asked her to say goodnight to Uncle Roe for me, and gave a cheery wave to everyone else at my table. I found my coat in the pile by the door, and I don't think anyone even noticed when I left.

Sometimes being mature really sucks.

The fire had gone out by the time I arrived home, and the ancient furnace was doing a poor job of keeping the house above sixty degrees. Cisco came bounding up to me with a plastic reindeer in his mouth, which meant Mischief had been into the Christmas decorations again. She was, of course, innocently relaxing behind the closed door of her crate, and I didn't even bother to wonder how she had opened a closed door and climbed up on the highboy to overturn the box of decorations again. I simply rescued the reindeer, cleaned up the mess, turned up the heat, and let the dogs out into the yard. Things are pretty bad when even the sight of Cisco with a reindeer in his mouth can't make me smile.

I checked the answering machine, and there were three messages: *Miss Stockton, this Jason Wells from Estate Assurance Investments and I have a matter to discuss with you that I think will be great interest…*Delete. *Merry Christmas from America's First Credit Card. Holiday bills getting you down? We'd like to help you out with our low, low interest rate of…*Delete. *Miss Stockton, this is Jason Wells from Estate Assurance again. I'd very much like to talk to you about this important opportunity…*Delete.

Well, what had I expected?

I put on water for tea and tried to restart the fire in the kitchen stove, getting a smudge of black soot on my new red dress in the process. That's when I had a temper tantrum. I kicked the stove door shut—getting soot on my silver shoe as well— and threw the poker at the iron stovepipe in frustration. The clatter was so terrible that it aroused the dogs into a barking fit outside, and I was ashamed of myself.

I started toward the door to calm the dogs, and the flash of bright headlights on the window made me realize it wasn't my temper tantrum they were barking about. The sound of tires roaring up the gravel driveway could be heard even through the closed windows, which meant the vehicle was going far too fast for safety. I felt a little lurch of alarm as I turned toward the front of the house.

I didn't make it out of the kitchen. A thunderous *BOOM* shook the house and I cried out and covered my head instinctively. Pots and pans clanged together in the overhead rack and cookbooks tumbled off the shelf. The teacup I had placed on the counter crashed to the floor. The dogs were going crazy in the yard.

I ran through the house and flung open the front door. There I stopped dead, staring. There was a pickup truck on my front porch, its steaming hood only inches from my torso as I stood on the threshold.

Worst Christmas ever.

TWELVE

I called 9-1-1 and rushed back out into the cold to try to help the driver. I had to climb over the hood to reach the driver's side door and lost one of my silver shoes in the process. The air bag had deployed, and I could see him struggling with his seat belt while trying to wrestle the air bag away. His face was bloody.

"Just take it easy," I called to him as I clambered over the porch railing and dropped to the ground. "An ambulance is on its way."

I discarded the other shoe and pulled myself back up onto the step, wrenching the door open. Lester Stokes turned on me with blood-shot eyes and a bloody nose and enough bourbon on his breath to knock out a camel, and he roared, "Where is he? Where is that lying, meddling, no-account husband of yours?"

He stumbled out of the truck, almost knocking me into the boxwoods that lined the porch. "And you too, you worthless slut!"   I reeled backward, both at the insult and at the danger posed when Lester, holding on to the door handle, swayed toward me. "You got no business nosing around my place, getting my boy locked up, when we ain't never done a damn thing to you! Not a damn thing! Well, I'm here to teach that man of yours a lesson, and you too! I'm not afraid of no law, I'm not!"

I'm no fool, and unless one of my dogs is in danger, I have absolutely no problem resisting the urge to play the hero. When a crazy drunk tries to drive his truck through my house and then stands in my yard threatening me, I'm not in the least embarrassed to hightail it back inside and lock the door. And that's exactly what I did until I heard the sound of sirens and saw the flash of blue and red lights four minutes later. By that time I had brought the dogs inside and locked them in the study, and had even taken a moment to find ammunition for my daddy's deer rifle, just in case. I didn't have occasion to load it, though. Lester was too drunk to climb back up the steps to the house, so he just stood out in the yard yelling at me until the police car, followed closely by an ambulance, pulled up beside him.

I pushed my feet into a pair of work boots and my arms into my coat sleeves, and I went out the back door and around to the front. By the time I got there the paramedics were leading Lester toward the open doors of the ambulance, and Mike Denson, one of the deputies who had drawn duty tonight and had therefore missed the party, was gazing up at the pickup truck that was half-on and half-off my porch, scratching his head.

"Quite a mess you got there, Miss Stockton," he said.

"You could say that." I thrust my hands into my coat pockets, shivering as I cast an uneasy glance over my shoulder toward Lester. The lights from the open ambulance flooded my lawn, and the paramedics were trying to get him to sit down so that they could examine his injuries.

"Lucky it didn't go through the wall. Somebody could have been hurt."

"Somebody could have been hurt anyway!" I objected incredulously.

"No doubt about that," he agreed. "Doesn't look like there was any structural damage, though, except to your steps. You want me to call a wrecker and get that thing out of here?"

"Yes!" And then, regretting my sharp tone, I added more reasonably. "Listen, Mike, whatever you do, don't call the sheriff out on this. He's at the Christmas party, and..."

Mike looked at me regretfully. "Sorry, Miss Stockton, you should have told the dispatcher. It's pretty much protocol to let an officer know when a call comes in from a member of his family."

"But I'm not his family!"

Mike just said again, "Sorry. Let me get the wrecker on its way out here and then you can tell me what happened, okay?"

Buck arrived just as I finished giving my report to Mike, followed closely by Uncle Roe and Aunt Mart. I hated that. Aunt Mart couldn't hide her alarm when she saw the state of my porch and fussed over me like a hen with one chick even though it was clear I was unharmed. Uncle Roe was fascinated by the engineering aspect of the truck-on-the-porch situation, and Buck, after a brief, "You okay?" to me, went off to interrogate Lester.

"The trouble with this town is there's too much drinking," declared Aunt Mart with a scowl. "We were all a lot better off when we were a dry county."

"Now, Martie," said Uncle Roe, perhaps in light of the fact that he had just come from a party where at least three quarters of the sheriff's department had had more than one beer, "you know it's not the drink, it's the drinker. Besides, people would just be going over the county line to buy their liquor if they couldn't get it here, same as they've always done."

I said, "I'm sorry you had to come all the way out here, and leave the party, too."

Aunt Mart gave a dismissive wave of her hand. "The party was over. And I certainly hope you don't think we wouldn't come out for something like this. What in the world was the matter with that man, anyway?"

I pushed my cold fingers through my hair and muttered, "Oh, he's mad at Buck about something."

Uncle Roe gave me a knowing look, and I responded defensively, "It's not my fault his son is a petty thief and a pothead and chose to withhold information in a police investigation."

Pothead, of course was a little strong, and so was petty thief. I'd been guilty of equal if not greater offenses in my youth, but the great advantage of adulthood is that the mistakes you make as a kid no longer count. Or at least they shouldn't.

Still, I was feeling a little huffy as I finished, "Besides, I never would have gotten involved if it hadn't been for the puppies. And it's not my fault that Lester Stokes won't spay his dog! I'm going to see what's going on," I finished uncomfortably and trudged across the yard.

The paramedics had cleaned up Lester's face and put a strip of tape across the bridge of his nose, which was purple and misshapen and appeared to be broken. Apparently they'd given him some B-12 and oxygen as well, because he seemed a bit more sober than he had been the last time I'd seen him. He was sitting on the back of the ambulance with a cold pack pressed against his face, with Mike looming over him on one side and Buck on the other.

"So here's what we're going to do," Buck was saying when I walked up. "We're going to take you to the E.R. to get checked out, and from there you're going directly to jail. The charges are reckless conduct, driving under the influence, making terroristic threats, vandalism, public endangerment..." he glanced at Mike. "Did I forget anything?"

"Failure to properly maintain a vehicle," supplied Mike helpfully. "Busted taillight."

Buck nodded and turned back to Lester. "And oh, yeah, assault with a deadly weapon. I hope you didn't make any plans for Christmas."

Lester's head shot up. "What are you talking about, what deadly weapon? I didn't assault nobody!"

"You tried to drive a two-ton pickup truck into a residence with the intent to harm the person inside." I felt a little sick, just hearing Buck say that. "That's assault with a deadly weapon and you're looking at twenty years, my friend."

I swallowed hard, and so did Lester. He said, "I told you, my foot slipped. I never meant to drive the truck in the house."

Then he looked at me and his rheumy, swollen eyes looked a little desperate, if still defiant. "I never meant you no real harm, you gotta know that. If I had I wouldn't've used a truck, and you wouldn't be standing here."

"Wrong answer," Buck said coldly.

"You shouldn't have come around messing with my family!" Lester said, now angry again. "You and that damn dog of yours—"

"You leave my dog out of this," I said with a sudden lurch of alarm.

"You don't mess with my family," he repeated belligerently.

Buck looked at him with eyes like steel. "And you don't mess with mine."

He jerked his head toward Mike. "Read him his rights. Go with him to the hospital. Make sure he gets what he needs. And don't screw this up. If he gets out of jail one day before his sentencing it'll be your ass."

"Yes, sir."

Buck touched my shoulder and turned me away as Mike pulled Lester to his feet and put the cuffs on him. I felt my eyes well up because Buck had called me family, and then I was angry because I wasn't his family and this was mostly his fault, anyway. None of this would have happened if he hadn't let Cisco go pretending to be a drug dog.

Almost as though reading my mind he said, "Honey, I'm so sorry. I never should have let you get involved."

"You didn't 'let' me do anything," I returned and stretched out my step to move away from his hand on my shoulder as we walked toward the house. The tow truck drivers were hooking up a chain to the back of Lester's truck while Uncle Roe supervised, and there was a lot of shouting and chugging of engines. "You're not really going to charge him with assault with a deadly weapon are you?"

"I'm damn sure going to try," he replied grimly. "We can't have people thinking they can take out their grudges with the law on police officer's families. Not for one minute."

I stopped and turned to look at him. "I'm not," I said distinctly, "your family."

There were about a half-dozen different emotions that flickered across his eyes in that moment, and I couldn't read any of them. Or maybe I just didn't want to. Finally he said, "You know what I mean." And started walking again.

"He had to put up his house to make Nick's bail," he said after a moment. "That's probably what set him off. How much damage do you think you've got?"

"Go home, Buck," I said.

He stared at me.

"You're not on duty, the situation is under control, and you've got company." My voice was tired. "Just...go home."

His brows drew together slightly. "Are you mad at me about something?"

I sighed. "No. I'm not mad. You can be a jerk sometimes, but you can't help it. All I want to do is go to bed."

He turned away, still looking puzzled, and I couldn't stop myself. I said, "How long is she staying?"

He looked back at me and had the grace to look uncomfortable. "The weekend."

"Good night, Buck."

I stood shivering in the yard with Aunt Mart while the ambulance pulled away and Buck's car followed.

The tow truck pulled Lester's pickup off the porch with a great deal of creaking and grinding and left big scars across my driveway as it lumbered off. Uncle Roe examined the damage and declared it to be relatively mild.

"They just don't build houses like this anymore," he pronounced with satisfaction. "You're going to have to get somebody out here to rebuild the steps, but then you'll be good as new."

Aunt Mart tried to persuade me to come home with them, but I assured her there was no need. I was fine.

She looked at me skeptically. "Are you sure? You don't look fine."

"I just don't understand why people have to be so mean," I said miserably, thrusting my hands deep into my coat pockets and suppressing another shiver. "I thought we had good neighbors. At the Christmas parade everyone was laughing and singing, and then somebody abandons a baby in the cold, and somebody else kills a man, and then somebody dumps a box of puppies by the side of the road, and then somebody tries to drive his truck through my house. It's Christmas. It just doesn't seem right."

My aunt looked at me with eyes filled with compassion, and I thought she probably understood why I was really so sad. She hugged me hard, advised me to have a cup of warm milk and go straight to bed, and left with Uncle Roe.

I was so emotionally and physically exhausted that I didn't even bother to put the girls in their crates. I didn't take off my makeup or brush my teeth. I just shucked off my ruined red dress in the dark, left it lying in a puddle on the floor and crawled into bed with the covers pulled up over my ears, letting the tears leak out onto my pillow. Eventually I felt the featherlight weight of an Australian shepherd land on one side of my feet, and then on the other. I didn't even bother to reprimand them.

But then the bed creaked with a heavier weight, and I pulled the quilt away from my face and looked over my shoulder. Cisco's eyes, catching the reflection of ambient light, looked up at me balefully from the foot of the bed. He was lying flat on his belly, head down and paws out, as though he thought he could blend in with the covers. As I watched, he started to belly-crawl toward me.

"No dogs on the bed," I said thickly.

He stopped dead, trying to make himself invisible.

I turned my head back to the pillow and closed my eyes.

Cisco inched his way alongside me until his head was beside mine on the pillow. I stretched out my arm around his shoulders and fell asleep with my face in his fur.

What the hell. It was Christmas.

If you are ever feeling lonely, blue or out-of-sorts at Christmastime, here's what you do: put an ad in the paper and on the radio that says *Golden retriever/lab mix puppies ready to come home for the holidays. 8 weeks old, all shots. Adorable balls of fluff! Small adoption fee.* And leave your phone number. I guarantee you won't have a minute to feel sorry for yourself until the last puppy leaves in the arms of its new Forever Mom or Dad.

As a general rule, our policy is not to adopt rescue dogs—particularly puppies—during the holidays. In the first place, people get such a sentimental notion about puppies under the Christmas tree with big red bows around their necks that they forget all about the puddles on the carpets, the chewed up furniture, and the standing out in the icy wind at two a.m. waiting for Puppy to finish his business. They make impulsive decisions that they would not have made any other time of the year. Secondly, the holidays are just too hectic around most households for a new dog or puppy to get the attention he needs, and a stressful environment like that is the worst possible way to welcome home a new member of the family. And of course we categorically discourage giving puppies as surprise gifts; very often the person who is surprised is the giver when their good intentions turn out to be completely unwelcome.

But rules were made to be broken, and Maude and I had decided that, with two weeks to go before Christmas and only three puppies to re-home, we would begin a screening process that would make sure all the puppies had homes by New Year's Day. The phone hadn't stopped ringing since.

I immediately eliminated any household with children under six. Puppies are not educational toys, and no mother of preschool children needs another responsibility on her to-take-care-of list. I also eliminated the frail, infirm, and those over eighty. These were going to be big dogs. I was left with a list of front-runners from whom Maude and I would choose who would be invited to come for a personal interview and to interact with the pups.

It was a brilliant Tuesday morning, with a sky so blue it practically hurt to look at it, and a rime of new snow on the high mountain peaks. My steps had been repaired and were awaiting the first day with temperatures above forty for paint. My kitchen smelled like coffee and the cinnamon rolls Maude had brought from the bakery in town, and a fire crackled in the wood stove—which was securely screened by a metal puppy gate, of course.

I sat on the kitchen floor and watched the puppies, temporarily released from their ex-pen, explore the big world of rag rugs, chair legs, and slippery polished floors. I defy anyone, no matter how sour he or she is feeling, to watch a puppy scramble to gain traction on a hardwood floor and not laugh out loud. Cisco lay beside me with his chin on the ground, determinedly pretending to ignore the puppies, even when one stopped by to chew on his tail or climb on his back.

His eyes, however, never stopped following them around the room.

Maude sipped tea at the kitchen table and carefully went over the list I had made of prospective puppy parents. "Jason Comstock," she said, striking through another name on the list. "Don't bother. He's only looking for a hunting dog." It's not that we had anything against hunting dogs, but our contract stipulated that the dogs we adopted must be pets only and live indoors.

I scooped up one of the little males who was trying to make a chew toy out of Cisco's ear, and turned him in the other direction. "What about that guy from Worley? He says he owns a garage and could take the puppy to work with him."

"Hmm." Maude sipped her tea. "A garage is not the safest place for a puppy, is it? But we'll see."

The female puppy placed a shy paw on my thigh and I cradled her on my lap. Doc had pronounced her clear of any deadly contagion and put her vitamins and liquid antibiotics three times a day. She already looked better, but was half the size of her brothers and I suspected would always have a more reticent personality. Early handling and proper socialization would do a lot to build her confidence, but she was not going to be the easiest puppy to place.

"This young couple from Asheville looks promising," Maude said. "But why would they want to come all the way down here to adopt a puppy?"

"They're just visiting relatives for a few days," I said. "That's how they heard about us. The husband wanted to surprise his wife with a puppy for Christmas but I told him if he wanted to see the puppies both of them would have to come for the interview."

"It looks as though we have a nice selection here. Why don't you ring them up and ask them to pop round tomorrow morning. I can be here by nine or so."

I was surprised. It didn't take two of us to show a litter of puppies, and I had always handled this kind of thing by myself. "Since when do you not trust me to place a puppy?"

"Don't be absurd." She sipped her tea. "I should merely think that after what happened the other night you wouldn't want to have strangers mucking about when you're here alone."

"Oh, for heaven's sake!" I didn't know whether to be annoyed or touched. "In the first place, I don't need a babysitter. In the second place, it wasn't a stranger who tried to drive his truck through my house, it was a neighbor. And in the third place—"

My cell phone rang.

"Unless it's a retired veterinarian who also has a wall full of blue ribbons and is looking for a new dog to train to his OTCH, I think you can safely tell them we've placed the puppies."

I got to my feet, cradling the female puppy in one arm. "It's not a puppy call," I said. "They come on the landline." I found my cell phone on the kitchen counter and checked the caller ID. My heart actually skipped a beat and I quickly answered it.

"Hi," I said. "Please notice that I not only answered my phone, I answered it on the second ring."

But the voice on the other end did not belong to Miles.

"This is Melanie Young," she said, in a very grown-up, businesslike tone. "You need to come get me."

My brows drew together in puzzled alarm. "What?" I placed the puppy back in the ex-pen and latched the gate. She promptly sought out the fleece mat in the corner and curled up. "Where are you?"

"I'm at the Middle Mercy Hospital," Melanie said, "with my dad. I think he's dying."

And she burst into tears.

THIRTEEN

I left Maude with the puppies and ran out of the house, still pulling on my coat and digging in my purse for my keys.   I reached the emergency room twenty minutes later, having horrible flashbacks to the night of Uncle Roe's heart attack only two months ago, and of my own father's fatal stroke years earlier. I stopped by the nurse's station long enough to determine that Miles Young was not anywhere close to death, but that only calmed my racing heart and gasping breath marginally. I knew what it was like to be sitting in a hospital waiting room, terrified you were going to lose your daddy. I thanked the nurse briefly, got Miles' room number, and hurried down the hall to find Melanie.

She was sitting on one of the orange, hard-plastic chairs, still wearing her puff coat with her mittens on a string around her neck, swinging her feet.   For once she did not have her iPad. A young woman in the blue poplin uniform of a hospital volunteer was trying to interest her in one of those Chinese box puzzles, but Melanie was having none of it.

In dog training, demeanor is everything: tension, anxiety and anger go straight down the leash and will ruin your training program no matter how skilled you are at everything else. And because dogs live almost entirely on an emotional level, there's no point in trying to fake them out; they can see through you like a lace curtain. I suspect the same thing is true of kids. So I paused at the door and took a moment to get my composure, found an easy smile for my face and a relaxed posture for my gait, and went over to her.

"Hi, Melanie," I said. And to the volunteer I added, "I'm a friend of the family."

The girl smiled cheerily and got up. "Melanie has been great," she assured me with a little too much enthusiasm. "Just great. What a brave girl. And everything is going to be fine, isn't it, Melanie?"

Melanie did not reply.

I said, "Thanks for staying with her." I was glad when she left, and I think Melanie was, too. I took the seat she had vacated, clasping my hands between my knees and trying to look casual.

"How're you doing?" I asked.

Melanie looked up at me with eyes that were red from crying, and for the first time since I had known her, she looked like a little girl. "I want my mom," she said.

Of course my instinct was to put my arm around her and draw her close, but I didn't think that would be received in the spirit it was meant. So I said, "I'm sure it would be okay if you called her—"

She started shaking her head before I was finished. "I called her. She wouldn't come."

There was nothing I could say to that. Nothing in this world.

"Well," I said, trying for a change of subject, "I'm glad you called me."

She shrugged morosely. "You were number one on Dad's speed dial."

I was number one on Miles' speed dial. I know it was completely inappropriate, but I felt a glow that started at my toes and spread all the way to my cheeks at that, and I wanted to grin like a fool. I was number one.

I said, "Your dad's just fine, you know. He's just got a little bump on his head."

She stared stoically straight ahead. "I know that. I didn't think you would come if I told you that."

I smiled, sensing the brave lie. "The doctors want to take your dad upstairs to a room where he can rest overnight, but the nurse said we can go in and say hello to him before they do. Do you want to?"

She nodded uncertainly, and I put my arm around her shoulders as we walked down the hall to the examining room. The door was open and I could hear Miles's voice long before we reached him.

"And I'm telling you, doctor, thank you for your advice, but I won't be staying. I have a little girl who's waiting for me, and I'm just fine. Where do I sign?"

"Mr. Young, I cannot allow you to drive in your condition, particularly with a child in the car. Do you understand the danger if you should pass out at the wheel?"

The silence that followed was the opening I needed to tap lightly on the doorframe, and I have to confess, I was as relieved as Melanie when I saw Miles on his feet and almost fully dressed. There was a large gauze patch on his head and his left arm was cradled in a blue sling. He was struggling to pull the sleeve of a wool shirt over the other arm, and I have to admit I spent an inappropriate moment admiring his naked chest which, even with the angry blue bruise that was spreading over his left rib cage, was worth staring at. He had the physique of a man who wouldn't mind climbing on a roof and swinging a hammer if he had to, and I liked that.

Melanie ran into the room and flung her arms around his legs. He exclaimed, "Hey sweetheart!" and hugged her with his good arm, but the enthusiasm of her embrace cause him to stagger back against the examining table and the doctor, a middle-aged woman with broad shoulders and a grim expression, quickly caught his arm to steady him.

"Dizziness, nausea, disorientation, loss of consciousness, coma," she said. "Reconsider what's best for the child."

I said, "It's useless to argue with him, doctor. His stubbornness is legendary. Really, Miles," I added. "On the bunny slope?"

He noticed me for the first time. "Raine?"

"Melanie called me," I said, coming into the room.

"Thank God," he said, easing himself gingerly into a sitting position on the examining table. "I thought I was hallucinating, which would mean I really am as bad off as these idiots think I am." Melanie climbed up beside him and settled in the crook of his good arm, and he gave her a squeeze. "Good thinking, Mel. I knew I could count on you."

The doctor looked at me. "Are you a relative?"

"Friend," I said, and I met Miles's eyes as I said it.

She looked at Miles. "Mr. Young, I am sending an orderly with a wheelchair and he'll take you up to your room. We'll help you make whatever other arrangements are necessary but this is not negotiable."

I said, "I think we've got it under control." And this time Miles did not argue.

"It wasn't on the bunny slope," he told me when she was gone. "I left Mel with her ski group while I practiced a mogul run and..." He looked wry. "I guess it's been a few years since I did that. Dislocated shoulder and concussion. They want to keep me overnight. It's hospital policy. Completely ridiculous, of course. Just a little headache."

It looked to me like the kind of headache that could kill a horse, and I casually went over and picked up the shirt he had dropped on the floor. "I hear they have really good pain meds here." He winced as I helped him slip his arm into the sleeve, and Melanie solicitously pulled the shoulder of the shirt over his bandaged arm. "But anyone can see you're fine."

"Did anyone ever tell you you're a smart-a..." He glanced at Melanie and smoothly finished, "Aleck?"

I smiled. "Constantly."

He said, "Thanks for coming."

"You're welcome. You know Melanie is welcome to stay with me," I added casually, "but if you'd feel better with someone more responsible in charge..."

"Hey," was all he said, but the look he gave me was enough.

I returned a smile that only pretended to be reluctant. "Well, okay then." Then I looked at Melanie. "What do you say? Girl party, right?"

She giggled just like a little girl, and Miles caught her hand and squeezed it. I thought the two of them could use some daddy-daughter time, so I said, "What can I bring you from the vending machine? Name your junk food."

Miles ordered cola and Melanie ordered an orange drink and chocolate chip cookies—so much for her wheat allergy—and I left the room, glad to feel useful.

The vending machine on the first floor was out of orange soda, so I went up one to obstetrics/pediatrics. I was coming back down the hall toward the elevator with an armful of soft drinks and snack foods when I saw a familiar and unexpected figure—two of them, in fact—standing outside the nursery.

"Mrs. Holloway?" I said, and she turned.

Standing beside her, looking strained and bedraggled and not at all happy, was Ashleigh Lewis.

"Raine!" exclaimed Ruth Holloway. "I almost didn't recognize you without Cisco." Her face was radiant and her tone almost giddy. "You'll never believe what's happened. Oh, I'm sorry, Raine, this is Ashleigh." She touched Ashleigh's shoulder and then smoothed back her hair gently. "Ashleigh is staying with us until her situation is settled."

I wondered if Ashleigh knew I was the one who had discovered her hiding place, decided there was no way, and said, a little awkwardly, "I'm so sorry about your father, Ashleigh."

Ashleigh cast down her eyes and didn't answer.

"Ashleigh's not going to be our only guest over Christmas," Ruth declared, practically bursting with excitement. "We're here to pick up Baby Hope—that's what the nursery staff named her and I think it's perfect, don't you?—the baby who was left in the Nativity manger! We're going to be her foster parents, and if all goes well..." She broke off, a little breathless. "Well, it does seem kind of destined, doesn't it? That Mary and Joseph should adopt the baby in the manger?"

I had to agree that it did seem appropriate, and I was happy for her, but I couldn't help feeling that this whole thing had to be kind of hard on Ashleigh: awkward, plump, unwanted, and now the odd girl out in a foster family love triangle. On the other hand, I had my hands full managing one incomprehensible child, so I said, "I think it's great that you're going to have so many people around your Christmas tree. I hope everything works out for you."

"Thanks, Raine." She beamed, then said with a quick expression of concern, "No one is sick in your family, I hope?"

"Just visiting a friend," I assured her. "Merry Christmas."

She wished me a Merry Christmas back, and Ashleigh never lifted her eyes from the floor.

We stayed to see Miles settled in his room, but I could see his macho act was just that—an act—and I was reminded that people generally weren't in the hospital for the fun of it. I gathered up the remnants of our snacks and tossed them in the trash can, then said, "Okay, Melanie and I are off to do some serious damage to this town. We'll call you tonight. Get some rest."

Miles kissed Melanie's cheek and hugged her tight before she scrambled down from the bed, and then he held out his hand for me. "Come here," he said.

He looked a little pale and tired, so I took his hand. He said, "About what I said the other day... I'm sorry. I was an idiot."

"Yes," I agreed, "you were." I hesitated. "And you were also right. I'll do better next time." And then, because I didn't want the moment to get too sentimental, I said briskly, "What do you need me to pick up from the lodge? How are you getting your car back here?"

He said, "You don't have to do that. I'll get someone from the lodge..."

I said, with severely lifted eyebrows, "Excuse me? Melanie has been without her iPad for at least four hours that I know of, and we're coming up on an emergency here. Give me your room key. I'll take care of it. That's what neighbors do. Besides ..." I smiled at him. "It's Christmas."

He lifted his hand to my neck and made as though to draw me down to him, and I was sorely tempted, believe me. But I thought, *Head injury, child watching*, and I caught his hand and kissed his fingers lightly. "Rest," I advised. "I'll see you tomorrow."

I turned to Melanie. "Come on, kiddo, let's hit the road. I've got puppies to feed."

Of course the mention of puppies was all it took to erase whatever uneasiness Melanie had about leaving her father, and she hurried me along impatiently as I secured Miles's room key and instructions. We were out of there before the eleven o'clock lunch carts rolled down the hall. Allowing for a brief stop at Taco Bravo on the highway, we had gathered all of Melanie's and Miles's possessions from the ski lodge, made arrangements for his car to be delivered to his house, and were safely back at my house being mauled by an excited canine crew by 2:00 in the afternoon.

There was a note from Maude: "Puppies out at 12:45. Three calls, none qualified. Set up interviews beginning at 10:00 a.m. tomorrow. Will arrive at 9:30." Then there was a P.S.: "Don't concern yourself with the Stokes dog; I'll take care of it."

What can I say? That was Maude.

"Hey," Melanie said, pausing at the entrance to the living room as she wove her way between two Aussies and a pushy, affectionate Golden toward the back of the house. "Why are all your Christmas decorations in your dog's cage?"

Sure enough, Mischief had finally managed to drag the entire cardboard box of Christmas ornaments off the highboy, out of the dining room, and somehow had wedged it halfway into her crate. A trail of red ribbon, glitter garland, and miniature lights marked her trail through the house, and blue and green and red and silver Christmas ornaments spilled from the open lid of the box onto the floor in front of the crate.

"Oh," I said, "that's just Mischief's idea of a joke." But I stood with my arms folded across my chest in complete bafflement, trying to figure out how she had done it. And once she pulled the box into her crate, how had she managed to climb over it and be waiting for me at the door when I got home?

"Dogs don't make jokes," Melanie said skeptically.

"This one does." Then with a helpless little shake of my head, I abandoned the effort of trying to understand the wiles of my dog. "Come on, let's take the puppies out."

The clumsy, comical antics of three fuzzy puppies worked their magic on Melanie just as they had on me. While the three older dogs raced around the play yard, practically shouting *Look at me! Look at me!* Melanie had eyes only for the puppies. She picked them up and turned them around when they started to stray out of their safe zone and into the big dogs' play yard, she laughed out loud when they tripped over their own feet while chasing each other and face-planted in the grass. When the two bigger pups ganged up on the little female, Melanie stepped in and scooped her up protectively. I have to admit, as crazy as it sounds, I saw a little bit of myself at that age in her when she did that.

I got some leftover chicken from the fridge and a clicker from the basket of training supplies on the back porch, and spent a few minutes demonstrating the rudiments of clicker training to Melanie. People are always asking me when is the best time to start training a dog, and my answer is: as soon as he's born. Puppies' brains are like little sponges—just like children's—and while they are young and eager to learn everything about the world and their place in it, there is absolutely nothing you can't teach them. Melanie was a quick learner, too, and within two minutes had all three puppies lined up in perfect "sits" before her, eyes watching her expectantly to discover what else they could do to earn a treat. She was grinning from ear to ear with her newfound importance, and so was I. Kids make the best clicker-trainers for two simple reasons: timing and coordination. Thanks to the video game industry, children today are practically born with those skills.

"You can teach a puppy anything you want," I told her, "as long as you let him know with the clicker when he's done something you like, and reward him with food for doing it. But the clicker is powerful tool, and you can't treat it like a toy. Remember — the first time you click without giving a food reward, it's like lying to the puppy. You've broken his trust. So when you run out of treats, what do you do?"

"Put the clicker in my pocket," she replied solemnly, memorizing every word I said.

"Right." I was starting to think I might be better with children than I'd been giving myself credit for. "And it's also important never to make learning seem like a chore, so we always stop the training session while the puppy is still having fun. That way they'll always be excited when they see the clicker, okay?"

She assessed the three waiting puppies and decided, "Okay, I guess they've learned enough for a while."

I said, "Good call. Let's take them back inside and let them have some nap time."

I gathered up the two males, and she picked up the female. "How long do they have to nap?" she wanted to know.

"A couple of hours."

"Okay. I think I'll teach them to shake hands, next."

There's nothing like the confidence of someone who has never discovered that failure is an option, and that's something you only find in kids.

I gave Melanie the responsibility of putting the puppies in their ex-pen and making sure the door was latched while I brought the older dogs in from the play yard. I was proud of myself for having discovered something that would take her mind off her dad—and her mom, for that matter—but when she seemed intent on pulling up a chair and watching until the puppies fell asleep, I realized I needed to come up with another plan.

"You know what we need to do?" I declared suddenly. "Get a Christmas tree!"

Melanie looked reluctant. "Do you think it's okay to leave the puppies alone?"

"Sure, they'll be fine."

"What if the big dogs break into their pen and step on them?"

I thought her concern was sweet, so I didn't point out that since that hadn't happened so far, I didn't think it was likely to. I said, "We'll take Cisco with us and put the Aussies in their crates. But you'll have to help me put the Christmas decorations away some place safe in case Mischief gets out again."

"Why don't you just put a lock on her door?"

"I've tried that. She always figures out how to open it."

"You need to find one she can't open."

"I know. But first I need to find out how she's getting out in the first place."

Melanie was thoughtful as we dragged the box of Christmas ornaments out of Mischief's crate and repacked it. I decided the only really safe place for the box was on the front porch, so I carried it outside while Melanie put on her coat again.

"You know," she said when I returned, "if you really wanted to know how she was getting out, you could set up a camera while we're gone. Like the security camera we have at my house in New York."

I raised an eyebrow, impressed. "Good idea," I said. "Only one problem. I don't have a camera."

She grinned. "I do."

It only took a few minutes to set the trap. Melanie engaged the video function on her iPad and I set it up on the mantel opposite the dogs' crates, high enough to give a pretty good view of most of the room. Mischief and Magic watched with such interest that I actually became a little nervous that Mischief might find a way to escape her crate and turn off the camera—or, more likely, knock the tablet off the mantel and break it. I therefore double-checked the slide bolt on her crate and even secured it with a plastic cable tie. She had chewed through the cable ties before, but it might buy us some time.

I said, "Don't get your hopes up. It's going to take her awhile to figure this one out."

"Don't worry," Melanie assured me. "It's just like the magicians on TV—they always double-lock all the chains just to make it look harder to escape than it is. But he always does it anyway."

I didn't know whether to hope she was right, or hope she was wrong.

With Cisco belted in the back seat and grinning happily to be going on a ride, we started down the road toward Walt Akers Christmas Tree Farm. Of course I missed the old days of hiking through the woods with my dad, a couple of dogs bounding ahead, finding the perfect tree and watching the woods chips fly as he cut it down with an ax, then getting sap all over my hands as I "helped" drag it back home. But the Christmas tree farm was almost as much fun, and probably more environmentally responsible, given the fact that there were a good many more people tramping around in the mountains looking for Christmas trees these days than there used to be. Also, there was something to be said for having a crew wrap your tree in netting and secure it to the top of your vehicle for you.

Walt had twenty-five acres planted in evergreens, and every year he opened a different "cut your own" section at the top of the mountain. At the bottom of the mountain, he had set up a flat acre of already-cut trees, and there were five or ten people browsing through that area already. The number would triple on the weekend. I stopped by the frame shack that served as the pay station and turned over twenty dollars for the cut-your-own option. I picked up a hand saw from the supply in the bin, and Melanie, Cisco and I drove up the dirt road that was marked by arrows toward the top of the mountain.

"Are you really going to cut down a tree by yourself?" Melanie asked.

"Not a big one," I assured her. "Besides, they have guys up here to help us."

She looked skeptical. "It would've been easier to get one that's already cut."

"But not as much fun."

"My mom always has a tree decorated from the florist delivered to our apartment."

Jeez, I thought, how *much alimony does Miles pay, anyway?*

"Last year it had peppermint candies and red and white roses on it. The roses turned black before Christmas though, and the candies melted."

I gave a noncommittal, "Hmm." then added, "On my tree I mostly have dog bones and shiny balls. They have a long shelf life."

She gave me a look—the kind that said she wasn't quite sure if I was teasing her or not, but if I was, she wanted to make sure she got it—and then she said, "Do your puppies have names?"

"They're not my puppies," I reminded her. "They're probably going to go to their new homes tomorrow, so no, I didn't name them. I think the person who is going to take care of them forever should do that."

She thought about that for a moment. "I don't know how you can be a puppy's mom for a little while, and then just give it to somebody else."

"It's not easy," I admitted. "Sometimes I can't do it. Mischief and Magic were rescue dogs, but I couldn't give them away, so now they live with me. My collie, Majesty, was a rescue dog, and she lived with me for three years. I let her go live with my Aunt Mart because my aunt needed a dog, and that's where Majesty wanted to be. But Mystery, the border collie, was a rescue dog too and she *never* wanted to stay with me—so now she lives with my friend Sonny, which is where she wants to be. The same with Hero, Sonny's service dog. I would have loved to have kept him, but he had a job to do, so he went to live with someone else. When you do the kind of work I do, you have to believe that there is a person for every dog, and a dog for every person, and that eventually the two will find each other."

That was probably a little too philosophical for a nine-year-old, but then again, what do I know about kids? Melanie seemed to accept it, and was quiet until we reached the parking area at the top of the mountain. And then she said, looking around, "Wow. That's a lot of trees."

I said, "Walt ships trees all over the state, and even down to Georgia and South Carolina. But if you really want top choice, you have to come up here and cut it yourself."

Spruce, fir, and white pine were planted in neat rows as far as the eye could see, ranging in size from four to ten feet tall. A person could spend days wandering through the grove, looking for the perfect tree, and there were certainly worse ways to pass the time. However, with only an hour or two before dark, I hoped we would find the perfect tree in a considerably shorter amount of time.

There were a few other vehicles in parked in front of the metal-roofed pavilion where the tree netter was, and a few more had driven down some of the wide lanes between rows. An attendant in a plaid jacket and an ear-flap hat was manning the pavilion, and other employees in orange vests were moving up and down the rows, helping people cut their trees. I decided to confine our search to the rows nearest the parking area. I dropped my cell phone in my coat pocket—I wasn't taking any chances on missing a call from Miles this time in the unlikely event that he tried to reach me—and got the saw from the back seat.

"Okay," I told Melanie, snapping on Cisco's leash. "We're looking for a tree twice as tall as you are, and about three times as wide."

"There are a lot of trees that size," Melanie pointed out, glancing around.

"Good, then it should be easy to find one." I released Cisco from the car and told him to sit while I zipped up my jacket against the cold wind that blew across the mountain. I wished I'd brought a hat.

"Do they allow dogs up here?" Melanie wanted to know.

"Sure, as long as they're on leash." I released Cisco from his sit and he immediately started sniffing the ground, excited to trace down every nuance of the scent of every man, woman, child, dog, rabbit, squirrel and deer who had trod the ground in the past week. The mountaintop probably resembled a tracking training field to him, and as I looked around, I wondered if Walt would let the tracking club use this area in off-season for practice. We were always looking for unfamiliar places to set up new challenges for our dogs, and they weren't all that easy to find, even in the mountains.

I called Cisco to heel, and though he seemed a little confused by the command—he clearly thought he had come here to track—he trotted along happily enough beside us as we started down the rows. When we came alongside the netting station the man in the plaid jacket straightened up and watched us with a hard look. He had a cigarette dangling from his lip and there was something uncomfortably familiar about him, but I couldn't quite place it. The way he kept staring at Cisco, I thought he probably had something to say about having dogs on the premises, and sure enough, he did. But it wasn't what I expected.

"Hey," he said. The cigarette bobbled when he talked. "You're that woman with the drug dog, ain't you?"

It took me a moment, but I recognized him from the trailer park, when everyone was milling around to pet Cisco while we waited for Buck to clear us to leave. I stopped, and Cisco, after a moment's thought, remembered his manners and sat by my side. I said, "Cisco is not a drug dog."

"Yeah?" He took the cigarette out of his mouth and his eyes narrowed as he looked at it. "I hear tell they got these drug dogs that can smell when something has just been touched by somebody that handled drugs. They'll go straight to it, every time."

I instinctively edged in front of Melanie; I'm not sure why. Maybe it was just to keep her from joining in the conversation. I said, "I wouldn't know. I don't train drug dogs."

"Hey, Dusty! Give me a hand with this twine, will you?"

He looked around at one of the men who was trying to secure a Christmas tree to the top of an SUV. He looked back at me and spat on the ground. "You gotta keep that dog on a leash up here."

"I will," I said.

He took a knife from the case on his belt and went to cut the twine. I released Cisco from his sit and he bounded happily into position beside me as we turned toward the row of trees that would take us the farthest away from the netting stand. I think he was still under the illusion that this was a tracking exercise. Whenever we stopped to examine a tree he would get his fill of sniffing the grass around it, and I didn't bother to correct him. The point was to make sure that everyone had a good time.

We found three or four trees that, in my opinion, would have served just fine. But the day was bright with late afternoon sun, the wind wasn't so bad in the shelter of the trees, and I enjoyed the walk. Melanie seemed to be having almost as much fun as Cisco was, wandering through the sweet smelling evergreens and turning a critical eye on every tree I pointed out and declaring it a "no way", a "maybe", or a "top three". Inevitably, we trekked much further away from the car than I had intended.

"Okay," I announced finally, "we need to make a decision now and start back home. We have to let the puppies out pretty soon."

The mention of the puppies was all it took to galvanize her, and she quickly chose the last tree we'd considered—which also happened to be the one that was farthest from the car. "You're sure?" I prompted.

"Positive."

"Because once I start cutting, it's ours."

"That's the one," she assured me importantly.

I handed her Cisco's leash and pulled on my gloves. "Okay, you keep an eye out for one of the guys in an orange vest to help us get it back to the car."

"Will do."

I positioned the hand saw and had started cutting before I realized she and Cisco were halfway down the row.

"Hey!" I called after her, straightening up.

"There's a guy over here," she called back, "on the next row. I'll go get him."

I saw it happen a split second before it actually did, and too late to prevent it. Cisco's ears went up, his nose went down, his tail swung excitedly, I cried, "Watch the"—and Cisco sprang away from Melanie before I could finish, "—leash!" He took off at a leaping bound, trailing the leash behind him.

Melanie cried, "Cisco!" I dropped the saw and started running, and so did she.

If I could ever have gotten a run like that out of Cisco on the agility course, I would have been a proud blue ribbon owner. He ducked and dashed in and out of the evergreens as though he was taking the weave poles at full speed. He sailed over stumps without breaking stride. Occasionally I would catch a glimpse of the cotton-tailed bunny that started the race, and I knew Cisco had about as much chance of catching it as we did of catching him. And the whole time my heart was in my throat because if he caught his leash on anything at that speed he would break his neck.

Generally I do not advise chasing a runaway dog, because the pursuit will only make him more excited about the keep-away game. In this case, however, as with every other time Cisco had gotten away from me on the tracking course, my goal was just to keep him in sight. He had no idea where he was, and when he finally did slow down, I wanted him to be able to find me.

Eventually we moved out of the cultivated rows and into the edge of a scrub brush and pine sapling tangle. There was a rusted-out silver Airstream trailer two or three hundred yards away, and Cisco was eagerly sniffing the ground in front of it. My guess was that the rabbit had gone under the trailer. I came to a stop and rested my hands on my knees, struggling to catch my breath. Melanie came up behind me a moment later.

"I thought," she gasped, "he was a trained dog."

I glanced at her. Her cheeks were bright red with exertion and her hair was wind-tangled and sweaty, just like mine. "He is," I answered, and added darkly, "Kind of." There was no denying the issue any longer: Maude was right. Cisco's lack of impulse control was a disaster waiting to happen. But maybe Sonny was right, too. Here he was in a place that looked exactly like a tracking course, and who could blame him for tracking? His skills were being under-used. I had no one to blame but myself.

I took one last deep breath and straightened up. "Okay," I said. "This is what I want you to do. Start walking up to him. When he looks at you, turn around and run back to me."

She looked at me uncertainly. "Why don't I just go get him?"

"You'll see."

Melanie gave me one more of her skeptical little looks then started plowing through the undergrowth toward the trailer. She probably thought that I sent her because I didn't want to get all covered with burrs, and she was partially right. The truth was that from that distance Cisco probably would have come when I called, but I saw no reason not to take the opportunity to share another lesson in dog training with her.

Just as I expected, Cisco looked up alertly as soon as he heard her approach. I called, "Remember, don't chase him. Make him chase you!"

Melanie took another couple of steps toward him, and Cisco play-bowed and yipped happily at her. She turned and started running toward me, just as she had been instructed. That was when Cisco double-crossed me. He spun around, play-bowed again, ducked to snatch something up from the ground, and then, *finally*, he raced after Melanie. I caught his leash as he reached her, and just before he jumped up on her in his signature "tag!" greeting.

"There aren't very many dogs who won't chase a running child," I explained to Melanie, reaching down to extract what appeared to be a dirt-smeared golf ball from Cisco's mouth. "So if you meet a strange dog and you don't want to be chased, what do you do?"

"Don't run," Melanie pronounced matter-of-factly. "What's that?"

I opened my hand and we both looked at the object Cisco had retrieved, which was not a golf ball at all, but the decapitated head of a cherubic-looking ceramic doll. Puzzled, I glanced back toward the trailer, which did not look like the kind of place a family with children might ever have lived, and then I stared more closely, startled. I could have sworn the door opened a crack, then closed as I watched.

The sun chose that moment to drop behind a mountain peak, and I felt a chill that was from more than the cold. I dropped Cisco's find into my coat pocket and touched Melanie's shoulder. "Come on," I said with sudden urgency. "Let's go."

FOURTEEN

The sun was just beginning its spectacular painted-clouds show over the purple-shadowed mountains when we arrived home. Melanie and I wrestled the tree, still carefully wrapped in its protective netting, onto the front porch so that we wouldn't have to do it in the dark, then hurried inside. A chorus of puppy yipping greeted us, and both Melanie and Cisco rushed to the kitchen to attend to it. The house, however, looked suspiciously as we had left it, and Mischief and Magic were resting in their crates with heads on paws, looking far too innocent for my comfort. My eyes darted this way and that, looking for signs of mayhem, as I went to let them out. The first thing I noticed was that the cable tie had been chewed through on Mischief's crate, and that both bolt locks were disengaged. The doors to both crates, however, had been pulled closed.

I stood before Mischief's crate with my arms folded, completely unimpressed. "Really?" I said, and she pretended to ignore me.

I released them both and they took off like twin shots. There was the usual pre-dinnertime chaos as I turned the bigger dogs out into the play yard and the puppies into a smaller, outdoor pen close to the house. Melanie of course wanted to go with them, and I told her, "Okay, but let's call your dad first. I told him we'd check in before dinner."

I reached in my coat pocket for my phone but came up only with a ceramic doll head. I tried the other pocket, and my jeans pockets. I groaned out loud. "I must have dropped my phone at the Christmas tree farm."

"Oh, well, guess we'll have to call him later," Melanie said happily, and let herself into the pen with the puppies.

Well, at least I'd found a way to take her mind off her dad.

The phone call was delayed while I fed the dogs, showed Melanie how to prepare the puppies' food, cleaned up the puddles inside the ex-pen and sanitized the rubber liner I used to protect my wood floors, then took the puppies out once more for their after-dinner bathroom break.

"It sure is a lot of work taking care of puppies," Melanie observed as we carried the puppies back inside.

"You got that right."

"I guess that's why my mom won't let me have one."

If there is one thing I've learned it is never, ever, try to influence a parent's policy on pet-keeping. The only way a dog, or a family, will ever be happy living together is if everyone involved is one hundred percent in favor of the arrangement. Otherwise...well, that's why we have animal shelters.

It was a shame, though. Melanie was one of those kids who really could have benefitted from having a dog in her life.

I said noncommittally, "Moms are usually right about these things. But," I added, watching the way she nuzzled the female puppy against her face before setting it down in the ex-pen, "you can always come visit my dogs. I have plenty."

That seemed to surprise her, and she gave me a smile that seemed almost as shy as it was pleased. "Yeah," she said. "Okay. Maybe I will."

I rummaged around in the freezer until I found one of Aunt Mart's emergency casseroles—the emergency being the kind that occurred almost daily around here, when I had nothing nutritious in the house to eat—and popped it in the microwave. While it heated I dialed the number of the hospital, asked for Miles's room, and handed the receiver to Melanie.

She told him about training the puppies and searching for the Christmas tree, and how Cisco had run away but she had gotten him back, and about Mischief breaking out of her crate and dragging a whole box of Christmas decorations inside it. She exclaimed suddenly, "Oh! We forgot to watch the video! Gotta go, Dad, love you, bye!" She thrust the phone at me and raced out of the room with all three dogs on her heels.

Miles said, "Sounds like you two had a big day."

"I think she's having a good time," I replied casually, but I was grinning. The difference between the girl I first had met less than a week ago and the girl who had just raced out of the room was monumental. "I guess it took her awhile to warm up to me. How are you feeling?"

"To tell the truth, I haven't had a hangover this bad since the spring break in Mexico I'll never remember."

"I thought you didn't drink."

"Now," he corrected. "I don't drink now. Mexico is why. But the upside is I'm all caught up on *The Real Housewives of New Jersey*. Ask me anything."

I laughed. "Listen," I said. "I lost my cell phone, so if you need me call me on this line. I know how you freak out when you can't reach me."

"Very funny." He hesitated. When he spoke again his tone was very serious. "Listen, I want to explain why I was so short with you the other day. I'd just spent the morning on the phone with Melanie's mother, and my lawyer. It turns out she's decided to stay in Brazil with her new husband. Our custody agreement specifies that if either of us takes up residence outside the U.S., full custody automatically reverts to the other parent. So that's what is happening. As of now, Melanie will be living with me. Permanently."

The silence between us practically echoed. Not only did I not know what to say, I didn't even know what he wanted me to say. In a moment he filled the void with, "Yeah, I know. It hit me like that too. I don't know how to be a full-time dad. I'm not even very good at being a part-time one."

I managed, "Miles, you're being a little hard on yourself. You haven't given it a chance yet."

"Well, I guess it doesn't matter, does it? I have to figure it out. It's just that there's a hell of a lot to figure out, and I wasn't prepared for this. So I over-reacted the other day when you were late, and I'm sorry."

I smiled into the phone, just a little. "You're forgiven."

"Thanks." Some of the tension in his voice eased.

"It's the least I can do, seeing as how you're in the hospital and all."

"The thing is—I haven't told Mel yet. Somehow I don't think she's going to be too happy about it."

"You don't know that." My protest sounded weak, even to my own ears. "Kids are resilient. You might be surprised."

"I thought the ski trip would give us a chance to get to know each other, and then I could sit down and talk to her... well, it didn't exactly turn out that way. Thanks for stepping in, Raine. I didn't expect it."

"Hey," I reminded him, "that's what friends do. Besides, I'm having fun." It was the truth, and no one could have been more surprised than I. "She's a good kid. I like her."

He said, "I don't suppose you've given any more thought to the conversation we had the other morning."

"You mean the one where you gave me an ultimatum."

"I mean the one where I made a suggestion."

I said casually, because I did not want him to know how very much I had thought about that conversation in the past few days, "I've come close to eliminating a couple of options."

"Care to give me a hint which ones?"

"You're welcome to start guessing."

"You know that headache I mentioned?"

"Right." The microwave pinged and I said, "So, are they springing you tomorrow? What time do you want us to be there?"

We had one of those back-and-forths about how he didn't need me to pick him up and he could make arrangements for himself, and I finally told him that I would call after I had finished with the puppy interviews in the morning and let him know what time I'd be there. Men, honestly. Sometimes they can be such babies.

Before I finished my conversation with her father, Melanie was excitedly calling to me to hurry up, and as I returned the receiver to its cradle and turned to get the casserole out of the microwave, she plopped her iPad in the middle of the table. "Wait, you've got to see this! It worked, it really did – look, I've got it all cued up."

I abandoned the casserole and sat beside her, peering at the fuzzy still photo of Mischief frozen in video with one paw out of her cage. The real Mischief and Magic crawled underneath the table, almost as though they knew what was about to happen. Cisco, for once completely innocent, sat beside me alertly, ready to pass judgment with the two of us.

Melanie pushed play and the screen sprang to action. Mischief edged out of her crate and went immediately to her sister's crate, tugging at the lock. I watched in a mixture of amazement and consternation as, after less than ten seconds' work, the second Aussie nosed open her door and wedged herself out, wriggling happily. I stared.

"Wait a minute," I said. "Replay that."

Melanie did, and I could hardly believe my eyes. "That's not Mischief," I said. "It's Magic!"

Melanie grinned. "I know, right? You never double-lock Magic's cage, so it's easy for her to get out and then open the other door."

"Holy cow." I sank back in my chair, amazed. "It was Magic all along."

"Watch this."

She pushed PLAY again and we watched as the two dogs scampered off, moving in and out of the frame, disappearing for long periods of time. Melanie fast-forwarded until suddenly Magic appeared again, carrying something in her mouth. "What is that?" I leaned forward for a better look at the oversized, ungainly object that she half carried, half dragged across the room.

"Looks like a box," Melanie said.

I leaned back again. "That's exactly what it is," I said with a small shake of my head. "It's a shoe box — the box the shoes Miss Esther gave me were in. Mischief — or Magic — took the shoes out days ago."

We watched as Magic placed the shoe box in Mischief's crate, then scratched around on the cushion until it was mostly covered. Mischief then got inside the crate, turned around a few times and plopped down. When she did, the door, which was open only enough to admit an Aussie-sized body, swung closed of its own momentum.

Melanie ran to the living room while I watched the recorded Magic casually saunter into her crate and settle down for a nap. I leaned down and found the real Magic resting her head on her paws beneath the table, and I glared at her. "You must think you're pretty clever, huh?"

She blinked at me and closed her eyes.

"Here's the box," Melanie said, returning. "It's kind of squished." She tried to straighten out the flattened corners. "Hey, there's some stuff in here." She pulled out a few scraps of yellowed tissue paper and handed me a manila envelope.

I undid the clasp and shook out the contents. There were a couple of letters addressed to Esther at a Los Angeles address and a zippered plastic bag containing a dozen or so souvenir postcards from the fifties. "Hey, look at this," I said, pulling out one. "It's a studio shot of Lassie." I gave a shrug and a half grin. "Maybe Magic is a fan." I repacked the items, reminding myself to call the nursing home tomorrow to see if they had a forwarding address for Miss Esther. I was sure she would be glad to have her letters back, even if the postcards were only souvenirs.

We ate a quick dinner while the puppies wrestled and tumbled in their ex-pen, and the older dogs settled underneath the table and pretended not to watch our every bite. I turned on the outdoor lights and let Melanie take the puppies out by herself, but I watched her from the kitchen window while I cleaned up the dishes. It took some doing, but I managed to convince Melanie to let the puppies have a well-deserved nap while we set up the tree.

I got a fire going in the living room fireplace, dragged the tree inside, and carried down more boxes from the attic. The dogs, sensing the excitement of something new in the air, scurried up and down the stairs with me, trying to peer into the boxes. With Melanie's help, I wrestled the tree into the stand, got it semi-straight, and cut the net. The dogs scooted back as the branches sprang out of their confinement and filled the room with the piney smell of Christmas, and Melanie clapped her hands and laughed out loud. We spent the next hour unpacking boxes and unwinding lights, and both Mischief and Magic sat back and watched with pleased expressions on their faces.

I hung four red velvet stockings embroidered with
the names Mischief, Magic, Cisco and Majesty over the
fireplace. I filled a bowl with red and green glass balls
and tacked a garland of dog bones and fake holly over
the doorway. I sat on the floor and carefully
unwrapped my mother's imported Italian crèche,
arranging the figurines on a snowy bed of cotton
batting beneath the Christmas tree.

"Aren't you worried the dogs will eat those?"
Melanie asked. She was hanging miniature ceramic
dog bones tied with red ribbons on the tree branches.

"They wouldn't dare." I unwrapped the delicately
painted porcelain manger and placed it toward the
front of the scene I was building. "Besides, I have
fence that goes around the tree, just like the one that
goes around the wood stove."

I had learned the value of that years ago, when I
came home after a party to find all my Christmas
presents shredded and one tired puppy asleep on a
chewed-up cashmere sweater. The fence might not be
the most attractive Christmas decoration, but it was
definitely better than the alternative.

I unwrapped two sheep and placed them behind
the manger and found the shepherd next. When I
unwrapped the next items—my own addition of a
ceramic collie, two Aussies, and a golden retriever—
Melanie giggled. "Those don't belong there."

"Who says?"

"There weren't any dogs in Bethlehem."

"I'll bet you a dozen dog biscuits Bethlehem was swarming with dogs. And even if it wasn't, no self-respecting shepherd would have tried to move his sheep to Bethlehem without a good herding dog."

"Oh, yeah?" Melanie's familiar skepticism was back. "And what about the golden retriever? I bet they didn't even have them back then."

"Well," I admitted, "you're probably right about that." I arranged the four dogs worshipfully at the foot of the manger. "But if there had been golden retrievers back then, they would have been among the first on the scene—probably helping the wise men carry their frankincense and myrrh."

I couldn't help being reminded of our town's living Nativity as I placed the camels and the donkey and the holy family: Mary, Joseph, and finally the cherub-faced Christ child. As I started to set the figurine in the manger I hesitated, thinking about Nick and the stolen baby Jesuses, and then I frowned a little, struck by something else.

"Okay, that's the last one," Melanie announced, stepping back to admire her work on the tree. "Can we let the puppies out now?"

"Sure," I replied absently. I followed her into the kitchen, and while she herded the puppies out into the back yard, I looked around until I found the ceramic doll head Cisco had picked up at the Christmas tree farm. The resemblance between the angelic face on the expensive, hand-painted figurine that belonged in my manger and the face on the cheap ceramic imitation was striking.

"Odd," I murmured out loud, but just then the back door opened and a stream of puppies came bounding in, while at the same moment three big dogs decided they wanted to go out.

I orchestrated the exchange, and Melanie asked, "Can I show the puppies the Christmas tree?"

As a general rule puppies and Christmas trees do not mix, and neither do puppies and fireplaces, which is why I had confined these three to the kitchen. But I was feeling festive, and how many more opportunities would Melanie have to enjoy the puppies *or* a Christmas tree? So I secured the fence around the Christmas tree and barricaded the fireplace with ring gating, supplied Melanie with a clicker and a handful of treats and decided to use this as a training opportunity. We formed teams of big dogs vs. puppies and played games of "fastest sit" and "fastest come". The puppies won almost every round (well, okay, sometimes I gave them a head start)—with the exception of the female, who was a little shyer and slower than her brothers, and who was so intent on trying to cuddle up next to Melanie that she often missed the command. We played until the puppies fell asleep on the floor from exhaustion and my ribs hurt from laughing. Cisco, Mischief, and Magic wanted the games to go on all night, but I knew when enough was enough.

"Okay, it's past these guys' bedtime," I told Melanie, scooping up one puppy under each arm. "Mine, too. We've all got a big day tomorrow."

Melanie picked up the female puppy and cuddled her under her chin. "If I had a puppy like this, you know what I would name her?"

"Noelle?" I suggested. "Holly?"

She shook her head.

"Christmas? Angel? Star? Prancer? Dancer?"

"Nope. I'd name her Peppermint, and call her Pepper for short. Because peppermints look sweet on the outside, but they're spicy when you taste them. And just because this puppy looks quiet on the outside doesn't mean she's not spicy on the inside. It would be nice if she had a name to remind her of that."

I looked at Melanie with newfound respect as I placed the two boys on their fleece mat inside the ex-pen. They immediately curled up together and fell asleep again. "You know," I said, "I think you're exactly right. That's a great name."

Melanie handed the puppy over to me. "Maybe we could tell people that tomorrow," she suggested. "Whoever adopts her, I mean."

"Okay," I agreed. "We'll do that." I placed the pup beside her brothers. She yawned hugely, circled once, and then collapsed bonelessly atop one of the boys, sound asleep. Melanie and I laughed, and we spent a few more minutes just standing there in companionable silence, watching them sleep. There's something about kids and puppies that can transform even the gloomiest holiday into something special. And all in all, this wasn't shaping up to be such a bad Christmas after all.

FIFTEEN

The telephone rang at 7:15 the next morning. It was barely dawn, and the grayish light that crept into my room was enough for me to see Cisco rise from his bed, stretch elaborately, shake out his fur, and trot over to my bed with an expectant look on his face. He knew that phone calls in the dark, more often than not, meant that he would be putting on his Search and Rescue vest and going to work. I really hoped that wasn't the case on this cold December morning, less than two weeks before Christmas.

I picked up the phone on the second ring and tried not to sound too groggy. The voice on the other end was not the one I expected.

"Is this the woman who always rises at the crack the dawn?"

"Miles?" I blinked, rubbed a hand over my face, and squinted at the clock again. "For your information, dawn hasn't cracked yet. Not in this part of the world anyway. Is everything okay?"

"Now it is," he assured me. "I'm on my way home—with medical permission, by the way. I just wanted to let you know you don't have to pick me up."

"Thanks for waking me up to tell me that. How are you getting home?"

"I found a driver."

Of course he did. People like Miles never had to worry about the inconveniences ordinary people face. Then I was ashamed of myself for the uncharitable thought, particularly when he asked with more than a touch of anxiety in his tone, "How's Mel?" He was just a dad who didn't want to waste any time getting back to his little girl.

"Still asleep. You weren't planning to pick her up now, were you?"

"Why not?"

"Well, we're doing puppy interviews this morning and I promised she could help. I think she was kind of looking forward to it."

"Oh." He sounded disappointed.

"I could ask her when she wakes up," I volunteered.

"No, that's okay. I just felt a little guilty about ruining her ski trip, but as long as she's having a good time, that's okay with me."

"Do you want to come for breakfast? I'm making pancakes."

He chuckled. "Thanks, I'll pass. I know your cooking, remember?"

"Your loss. For your information, pancakes are the one thing I actually know how to make."

"Well then, I might just have to take a rain check. Give me a call when Mel is ready to come home, okay?"

By the time we hung up I could hear the puppies whining downstairs, and only seconds after that, Melanie's feet were padding down the stairs. It was a quite a difference from the last time she had stayed over, and I couldn't help smiling as I watched her bossily usher the puppies outside.

Six dogs, one kid, and me: the odds were against it, but somehow dogs were fed and exercised, the puppies' pen was cleaned and sanitized, pancakes were made and Melanie and I sat down to eat them within the hour. The pancakes were excellent, by the way. I hoped Melanie remembered to tell her father.

"Don't you think the puppies need a bath before their people get here?" Melanie said, spearing another forkful of pancakes. "First impressions are everything, you know."

Cisco watched intently as I transferred another pancake from the platter to my plate and drizzled it with syrup. "They just had a bath at the vet's," I reminded her. "And it's pretty cold to be running around with damp fur."

"You've got a lot of blow driers."

"That's true, but remember the little one is still on antibiotics. We don't want to take a chance with her getting sick again."

She chewed silently, obviously reconsidering. "Maybe we'll just brush them and put bows on them."

Bows on puppies hardly ever work, for obvious reasons. But it's the thought that counts, and I didn't want to take the fun out of it for Melanie. "I have a grooming spray that will make their fur shiny," I offered. "All you have to do is spray it on while you're brushing them. And it smells good, too."

Melanie gulped down the rest of her orange juice. "I'd better get started. I want to take a picture of them and send it to my dad."

I set Melanie up with a soft-bristle brush, some grooming spray, and yes, a spool of red ribbon, and while she concentrated on her task I cleaned the kitchen and checked my e-mail. There were a couple of training questions from former clients, some advertisements from local merchants disguised as Happy Holidays messages, and the few pieces of spam that always managed to get through the filters. Aunt Mart had e-mailed me the photos from the parade and the Christmas party, and I took a minute to scroll through them.

The first photograph that came up was the family photo of Aunt Mart, Uncle Roe, Buck and me, and I spent much too long looking at it with a sad, hollow feeling in the pit of my stomach. Then, with a surge of impatience that was directed mostly toward myself—I was not going to let Buck ruin a perfectly good morning, after all—I clicked back through until I reached the photographs of the Christmas parade. There must have been a dozen pictures of Majesty, and if ever I had doubts about whether I had done the right thing by letting my girl go, moments like this dispelled them. There was Majesty posing with Aunt Mart, Majesty posing with an unknown number of children, Majesty in front of the sheep trailer, Majesty getting her hair done, Majesty doing her "Lassie wave" for the camera with the Nativity scene in the background, Majesty with her twinkle lights on, Majesty waving to the camera with the Christmas tree in the background... I backed up a couple of shots, frowning as I looked more closely and then got cautiously excited. It was hard to tell, but I was almost certain that the hunched-over, downtrodden figure in the background was Ashleigh Lewis.

She had a duffle bag over her shoulder and held it protectively against her body, and the more I looked at it, the more I became convinced the picture was of Ashleigh, and it must have been taken shortly after she had hitched a ride into town with Camo Man. The ladders were still up around the Christmas tree, and there was enough light to shoot without a flash, so I guessed it had to have been close to five o'clock in the afternoon. She had never given any explanation at all for why she had left the safety of her hideout to go downtown on Friday afternoon. What kind of girl runs away from home and then goes to watch the Christmas parade?

I went through the remaining photographs more carefully, and a couple of shots later—because one can never have too many photographs of Majesty preening for the camera—I spotted Ashleigh again, almost out of frame but definitely the same girl. There was something different about her this time, though. Where was the duffel bag? Even in a town this isolated from most of the ugliness of the outside world, an abandoned duffel bag at a crowded event would not have gone unnoticed, so I didn't think she could have simply left it behind. She must have given it to someone. But to whom? And why?

The phone rang, and I called out, "Melanie, will you get that? It's probably your dad."

I didn't have time to analyze the photos again this morning, so I opened up a new window and, after a brief moment's hesitation, addressed a message to Buck at the office. I wrote, *Is that Ashleigh in the background?* Then, for clarification, added, *Aunt Mart's Christmas parade photos.*

Melanie called, "It's for you. Some estate person."

All three dogs raced through the house, barking excitedly, and I knew Maude must have arrived. I called back, "Tell him I'm not interested!"

"Okay!"

Quickly, I selected the two photographs to attach and hit Send. I hurried to the door. "Mischief, Magic, Cisco! Sit!" They sat, two tailless butts wriggling, one golden tail swishing, all three panting with excitement. I gave them a stern look. "What's the matter with you? It's just Maude."

I opened the door, and immediately saw what the matter with them was. Maude was not alone. She had a leash in her hand, and at the end of the leash was a white-faced golden retriever. I stared. "Is that the Lewis's dog?"

"It is," she replied briskly, and stepped inside. The Golden accompanied her at a trot.

Cisco stretched out his nose to sniff and the Aussies were one breath away from breaking their sits, so I gave them a sharp, "Ank!" as a reminder. I let Maude and the Golden get well inside, close the door, and then I told the girls, "Mischief, Magic, crate." They darted across the room to their crates, which of course made me look like a super dog trainer. And if anyone wondered why I would keep two dogs who are borderline cat burglars, that's why. There is a definite upside to owning dogs who are at least as smart as you are.

Maude said, "All things considered, I thought it might be best if I followed up on the spay proposal, rather than you. So I went over yesterday afternoon to talk to Alice Lewis about it—women are always more reasonable about these things than men, in my experience—and she surrendered the dog to rescue. As I hardly need tell you, her husband is in jail and her son just made bond and may yet be charged with murder, so she had quite enough to deal with."

I stared at her. "They're going to charge Nick with Earl Lewis's death?"

"Mrs. Lewis seemed to think so. I rather feel bad for taking advantage of the situation, frankly, but one must do what is necessary. We have a signed surrender form, and this fine young lady has an appointment with the vet for spaying this afternoon."

"Well, what do you know about that? It's a Christmas miracle." I reached down to pet the new arrival, and Cisco whined, politely reminding me he was still sitting. "Okay, Cisco, release." He bounded onto all fours and wriggled his way over to greet the new dog.

"Speaking of which..." Maude glanced around the newly decorated room while the two dogs completed their circling and sniffing routine. "The place looks nice. I'm glad to see you finally got the Christmas spirit."

"I had some help." I glanced up to see Melanie standing at the threshold of the room with the female puppy in her arms, regarding Maude somewhat suspiciously. She had clipped a small red ribbon into the fur just above the puppy's left ear, and I had to admit, it looked cute. I introduced her to Maude, and added, indicating the golden retriever, "This is the puppies' mother. We'll be finding a new home for her too."

"No kidding?" She brought the puppy over to the adult dog and set it on the floor. "Wouldn't it be cool if they all went to a new home together?"

I assured her that was very unlikely to happen, and while Melanie waited expectantly for some sign of recognition between mother and daughter and Cisco spun and play-bowed and practically begged someone to notice him for a change, Maude said, "I hope you don't mind keeping her over the holidays. I know it's a bit to ask with the kennel out of operation, but I'll take over for you of course as soon as I get back."

"No problem," I assured her. "I can use the company. It looks like no one is going to be in town this Christmas except me and the dogs. Come on, let's get her set up in a crate while we do the puppy interviews. What's her name, anyway?"

"I believe they were calling her Lady."

"I don't think Lady likes her daughter very much," Melanie said and picked up the puppy resentfully. "She keeps pushing her away with her nose."

"Mother dogs are not like human mothers, young Miss," Maude explained patiently. "Once a pup is weaned, they don't feel it necessary to hover."

"Some human mothers I've met could take a lesson," I observed.

"That reminds me," Maude said, "have you heard the news?"

I led the way to the library, which had been temporarily pressed into service as a storage area for kennel equipment. "Which news?"

"That poor baby that was abandoned in the manger was kidnapped. I heard it on the radio on the way over. Apparently it happened late last night or early this morning."

"You're kidding! Do you think the mother changed her mind?" And then I remember Ruth Holloway standing outside the nursery only yesterday, and the look of rapture on her face. My spirits fell, and I turned to look at Maude. "Oh, no," I said. "Ruth Holloway was the foster mom. Was the baby taken from her house? She must be devastated."

"I'm afraid I can't speak to the details. I'm sure your aunt would know."

Of course by then I was remembering the other person who had been with Ruth Holloway yesterday, and I was starting to get a very bad feeling. Hadn't Ruth told me Ashleigh was staying with her too?

I pulled out a portable crate and thrust it at Maude. "I'll help you set this up in a minute. I think I'd better call my aunt. "

Aunt Mart confirmed that the baby had been taken from the Holloway's home, and that Ashleigh, too, was missing. "It's been all over that blessed police radio this morning," she said. My uncle, even though he was retired, was unable to abandon his police scanner, and he kept it on at home almost around the clock. She sighed. "And it pains me to admit it, as much as I hate that thing, but I haven't been able to stop listening. What an awful thing to happen. I thought I'd go over to the Holloways with a cake this afternoon, as soon as all the police clear out. I know the poor thing must be a wreck."

"I think she may have had hopes of adopting the baby," I told Aunt Mart. "Do the police think Ashleigh did it, or are they looking at a double kidnapping?"

"Who knows what they think? Every man on the force is looking for her, though, and that little baby, so I don't imagine they'll get far, one way or another."

I wanted to talk more, but just then the doorbell rang, and our first prospective puppy parent arrived to a chorus of barking and yipping and the scurry of Melanie's very self-important footsteps across the room. It was a relief to put aside the remnants of kidnapping and murder for the happy mayhem of the hours that followed as a parade of prospective puppy owners lined up to ooh and ahh over the three shined, brushed and beribboned pups.

Adopting a dog from Golden Rescue is not a simple matter, nor is it with any reputable rescue group. We do a thorough interview over the phone, and if we can't verify the residence through references, we do a home visit. We keep a detailed application on file and require every adopter to sign a contract that specifies how the dog will be cared for, when he or she will be altered, and that he will be returned to us if the family finds itself no longer able to care for the dog. Our adoption fee barely covers the cost of first shots and the spay/neuter, but it's significant enough to make certain that new owners understand the value of their pet. We do follow-up visits and check with the veterinarian on record to make certain the spay or neuter surgery was performed on schedule. If it wasn't, we have the legal right to reclaim the dog. In other words, people who come to us for a dog understand in short order that this is a very serious matter. And in this case, they not only had to deal with Maude and me, but with Melanie as well.

Two people did not keep their appointments, one grew skittish when we showed him the contract, and another couple accidentally let slip what they had failed to reveal on the phone—that they intended the puppy as a gift for their three-year-old granddaughter, which was against our policy on several levels. Melanie grilled the remaining candidates as though they were applying for a government security clearance. Where would the puppy sleep? How close was the nearest pet store? What plans had they made for its education? Who would walk the puppy while they were at work? Did they own or rent? What did they plan to do with the puppy when they went on vacation? Maude and I had to smother smiles behind our hands as she marched each puppy into the room as though it were strutting down a runway, demonstrating its various talents and making certain to point out the weaknesses as well. For the most part, Maude and I merely supervised, and at one point Maude murmured to me, only half joking, "You really should hire that girl." For some reason, that made me proud.

Not surprisingly, most people gravitated toward the playful, husky males, and after protracted conferences, we agreed on good matches for both of the boys and sent them on their way. Melanie, of course, found room for improvement in both placements, but reluctantly agreed when we assured her our follow-up policy was uncompromising. As an unexpected bonus, the couple who was visiting from Asheville fell completely in love with the quiet, well-mannered Lady, completed the adoption form on the spot, and arranged to pick her up from the vet after her spay surgery was complete. But no one was interested in the female puppy.

"I don't get it," Melanie said with a frown when everyone was gone. "She's the best one. Why didn't anybody want her?"

"Well, a lot of people think female dogs are more trouble than males," I told her. "And she is kind of shy. Besides, she's still on medication, and maybe they didn't want to take a chance with a sick puppy."

"She's not sick." Melanie sounded defensive. "She's practically well. People are stupid."

"Sometimes," I agreed, "they are."

Melanie brightened. "Well, at least you get to keep her, right? She can be one of your dogs, and I'll come visit her."

I heard Maude chuckle at that, and I shook my head. "That's not the way it works, Melanie. My job is to find a home for her. I can't keep her."

"What happens if you don't?"

Maude said, "We work with rescue groups all over the South. We always find homes for our dogs."

Melanie looked distressed as she repeated, "All over the South?"

I said, "Don't worry, a puppy as cute as this will find her perfect home in no time. We'll put her picture on the internet and offers will come pouring in."

She didn't look very reassured as she picked up the puppy and carried it back to the now-empty ex-pen. "Even her mother's gone," she said sadly. The expression on her face as she gazed down at the puppy made me wonder how much she had guessed about what was going on between her own parents.

I tried to sound cheerful. "Come on, Melanie, get your things together while I call your dad. I know he's anxious to see you, and he's been so patient about letting you stay all morning."

She placed the puppy on the fleece mat and knelt down beside her, petting her. "It's no fun being the one nobody wants, is it?" she said softly. "Try not to get too lonely."

Maude and I exchanged a look that was sympathetic on her part, helpless on mine. I wanted to hug Melanie, but I didn't know whether she would welcome it, so I said instead, perhaps a touch too brightly, "Don't you worry about that. She's got a house full of dogs to play with, remember? Now let's leave her alone for her nap. I'm sure your dad will let you come play with her later."

Melanie latched the door of the ex-pen, but her step wasn't very lively as she went upstairs to get her things.

"It occurs to me," Maude murmured when Melanie was out of earshot, "that an ice cream treat wouldn't be inappropriate at the moment. It always used to cheer me up when I was a girl. Why don't you take her downtown to lunch?"

"That's a good idea," I said. The thought flitted across my mind that this would also give me a chance to stop by the sheriff's office—briefly, of course—and see what I could find out about the missing Ashleigh. "We'll have lunch at the drugstore counter. That's always fun and they've been advertising frozen hot chocolate from now until Christmas. I'll see if Miles feels like meeting us there. Do you want to come?"

"Thanks, but I've a full schedule of packing and shopping this afternoon. What do you suppose would be an appropriate bridal gift for a couple in their forties who've been living together for five years and who own a hotel?"

"Money," I assured her and picked up the phone to call Miles.

His phone went to voice mail, so I left a message. "Hey, it's me. I guess you're taking a nap. Melanie's feeling a little down after giving the puppies away so I thought I'd take her into town for lunch if it's okay. I was going to ask if you wanted to meet us at the drugstore but you probably need to rest. Anyway, I'll call you when we get there. No, wait—I forgot, I lost my phone. Listen, maybe I'll stop and see if anyone turned it in, so if you need anything, call Melanie on her cell. Bye." Then, because I didn't want a repeat of the last episode, I added, "It may be a couple of hours before I see you. Don't worry. Melanie will call you when we get to town. Feel better. Bye."

Melanie was marginally cheered by the prospect of frozen hot chocolate, and she really cheered up when, as we were pulling on our coats and gloves, I gave in to Cisco's hopeful gaze and decided to take him along for the ride. After all, he had been locked away all morning while people tromped through his house, and he had been relegated to the background ever since the puppies arrived. Maybe Sonny was right, and all he wanted was to feel special.

"Say, why don't we take the puppy too?" Melanie suggested eagerly. "I'll bet she'd like that! I was reading on the Internet last night that puppies should start getting used to car rides before they're twelve weeks old, and that you should take them fun places as often as you can so they don't think getting in the car means going to the vet. I think we should take her with us."

Maude gave me an amused look. "And who are we to argue with the Internet?"

I snapped on Cisco's leash and opened the door. "Well, that's all true, but it's too cold for her to sit in the car for as long as we're going to be gone. Cisco is a big dog with a thick coat. Besides," I added as I could see another argument forming, "I don't have a travel crate for her."

"She'll be lonely," Melanie protested.

I ushered her through the door. "She's got Mischief and Magic."

"But—"

"No more buts." My mother used to say that to me a lot. "You're getting a free lunch and hot chocolate. Live with it."

Melanie pouted as she fastened herself into her seat belt. "My dad is bossy, too. That's why my mom hates him. She says he's a control freak."

I darted a glance toward her. "I'm sure your mom doesn't really hate him."

"Yeah, she does. You should hear them fight every time he comes to pick me up." She shrugged. "That's why I started staying at school on the weekends. It was easier than listening to them fight."

I had no idea what to say to that. At all.

At noon on a Wednesday there were not many cars parked in the Christmas tree farm lot, and Walt was sitting inside the pay stand with his feet up, drinking coffee. When I asked if anyone had found a cell phone, he shook his head.

"I'm pretty sure I lost it at the top of the cut-your-own lot," I said, "in the weeds toward the back." I fished one of my Dog Daze business cards out of my pocket and handed it to him. "If anyone finds it, will you give me a call?"

He glanced at it and tucked it into a receipt pad. "Sure thing."

"You know," said Melanie, "if you left it turned on, we could call the number and maybe hear it ringing. That way you could just follow the ring."

I stared at her in amazement, and Walt grinned. "Smart kid."

"Do you mind if we go up there and try it?" I asked.

He waved us on with a "Good luck." And Melanie and I hurried back to the car.

There was only one attendant at the top of the lot — the dour-faced man who had been so interested in Cisco — and he gave us a hard look as we went by. I ignored him and followed the path past the parking area to the end of the lot, bouncing over the rutted ground until we reached the row where we had found our Christmas tree. My theory was that the phone had either fallen out of my pocket while I was cutting the tree, or while I was chasing Cisco. So this seemed like a good place to start.

Cisco was panting so excitedly at the sight of all the greenery — and very possibly remembering his happy bunny-chase — that I didn't have the heart to leave him in the car. I snapped on his leash and held onto it tightly as we started down the row of stately evergreens.

"Okay," I told Melanie, "let's start here. Dial this number." I gave her my cell number and waited until she had punched it into her phone, listening intently.

There was absolutely no one on the mountaintop but us. Brilliant puffy clouds drifted over a cobalt sky and the air was still and cold. There wasn't even enough breeze to stir the trees. I listened, and heard absolute silence.

Melanie shrugged. "Voice mail," she said, and disconnected.

"Okay, let's try over there."

We walked to the end of the grove, stopping every now and then to try again, and reached the brambly field with the trailer parked at one end of it. To my surprise, there was a beat-up, oddly familiar-looking pickup truck in front of the trailer today. I knew that Walt employed seasonal workers, and wondered if one of them might actually be living in that wretched place.

"Okay," I said, "if it's not around here, it's just not here. Let's give it one more try, then head back. I'm hungry."

Cisco pulled at the end of the leash, sniffing the ground intently, and I let him. Sometimes a dog just has to be a dog, and I was sure the ground was saturated with the smell of rabbits. Melanie dialed again, and I listened for the ring, but what I heard was not at all what I expected. The sound carried clearly on the cold air, and it was coming from the pickup truck.

Melanie said, "Sounds like a baby crying."

I said uneasily, "I think someone is living in that trailer."

I did not know why that should make me uneasy, but I recalled I had gotten the same bad feeling the last time I had been here. When you've worked with dogs as long as I have, the one thing you learn is to listen to your instincts. And my instincts now were making my scalp prickle.

"Come on," I said. "Let's get some lunch."

I started to turn, and then the door to the truck opened. A female voice, sounding a little frantic, called, "Nick, hurry up, can't you? The baby is crying! I think she's cold!"

I stared at the truck, suddenly realizing why it looked so familiar to me. The last time I'd seen it, it had been parked on my porch. And I saw the girl get out of the passenger door, holding a small, wailing bundle close to her chest. The breath left my body as all the pieces fell into place.

"Oh, my God," I said softly. "Ashleigh."

SIXTEEN

I turned quickly to Melanie. "Wait here," I said and started toward the trailer. But I hadn't taken a full step before it struck me: I was doing it again. I was accustomed to giving commands and having them obeyed and to going my own way without the encumbrance of someone who could not be counted upon to take care of herself. But I couldn't just leave a nine-year-old girl alone in a pine grove while I confronted a runaway and a possible kidnapper. I rethought quickly.

"Give me your phone," I said, and transfer Cisco's leash to her hand as I took it and dialed 9-1-1. "Come on, we've got to talk to that girl in the truck. Hold on to Cisco. Don't let him jump."

The dispatcher answered as we plowed through the weeds toward the trailer. "Rita, it's Raine. Listen, I'm at Walt Akers' Christmas Tree Farm, at the top of the cut-your-own lot. I can see Ashleigh Lewis. She's in Lester Stokes' blue pickup truck and it's parked in front of an old trailer in an empty field. I'm going to try to keep her here, but I need you to get a squad car out here just as quick as you can."

I was walked fast and Melanie huffed to keep up with me. "Is that girl a criminal?" Her eyes looked twice as big behind the glasses. "Are the police coming?"

Rita said, "Hold on a minute, Raine."

"I can't hold on! I–"

Cisco was starting to leap and lunge as we drew close to the trailer, and Melanie stumbled to keep up with him. I quickly disconnected and grabbed the leash, but Ashleigh had already noticed me. She tried to duck back into the truck but I increased my stride and called, "Ashleigh?" I drew Cisco into a sharp heel and leaned down to whisper to Melanie. "I'm just going to talk to her. Stay with me. Stay quiet."

"Hi," I said, trying not to breathe hard as I came up to Ashleigh, pushing aside the thorns and brambles that clung to my coat. "I'm Raine Stockton. We met at the hospital yesterday. You were with my friend Ruth Holloway, remember?"

She placed a protective hand over the baby's head and regarded me with a defiant look on her face, but her eyes were pure deer-in-the-headlights. Quickly they flickered from Cisco to Melanie and then back to me. I transferred the leash back to Melanie. "Wind it around your hand like I showed you," I told her. My eyes were on Ashleigh. "Keep him in a Sit. You're a good trainer. You can do it."

I gave Cisco the palm-out hand signal for "stay", and I took a few steps forward, watching Ashleigh. "You know just about everyone in this county is looking for you, don't you?" I said gently. "They think you kidnapped the baby."

Behind me, Melanie said. "Holy cow! A kidnapper."

The tiny wails were hiccupping with fatigue now, and Ashleigh pressed the baby closer, awkwardly swaying back and forth to soothe it. "I didn't kidnap anybody," she returned shrilly. "They can't take her!"

"I know that," I said and came closer. "You can't kidnap your own baby, can you?"

She looked at me with an awful flood of horror and guilt in her eyes, and she held the baby so tightly to her chest that tiny little choking sounds started to come from the depths of the blanket. I surged forward, but she released the ferocity of her grip and the whimpering became more ordinary. A big tear rolled down Ashleigh's cheek. She ducked her head to the blanket to hide it. "I didn't know," she said brokenly. "I didn't know what to do. I thought—I knew if my dad found out—I couldn't let him find out. I just couldn't."

She looked at me with eyes that were filled with torment, desperate for forgiveness, and I nodded with a slow and horrible understanding. The bloody sheets in the bleach-filled tub were not evidence of a murder, but of a birth. The phone call I had overheard, begging for help…

"You put the baby in the duffle bag," I said, "and sneaked her into the manger when no one was looking. What did you do with her while you were at school?"

"I put her in my closet with the radio on in case she cried. I didn't know what else to do. It was warm and I wrapped her in lots of blankets. I didn't know what else to do."

My heart lurched at that, and she went on, "But I couldn't keep her there. I knew if my daddy came back, if he found her…Nick came and took us to his brother's house and he said we'd be safe there, but I didn't feel so hot, and I didn't have diapers or bottles or anything, and if anybody saw me buying them, or Nick either, they'd know, and I couldn't stay there forever, hiding. So I decided to leave her in town, where somebody would be sure to find her, and then I'd run away. I had my mother's wedding ring, I took it out of my daddy's truck the night before, and I thought I could pawn it for some money, maybe a bus ticket…"

"But you lost it in that hunter's truck. You stole his wallet."

She nodded miserably. "But there was only about fifty dollars in it. Nick said the sheriff was looking for me, and I didn't have enough money to run away…And then my dad was dead and it didn't matter anymore, don't you see how funny that is? None of it mattered anymore!" Her voice rose with hysteria and her eyes had a wild look. Behind me, Melanie had gone absolutely silent. I didn't dare look around to check on Cisco.

"But the police were so mean and I was so scared, and they said they had already put Nick in jail and they didn't even know what I had done yet...And then when Ms. Holloway took me in, and then when the county gave her my baby—*my baby*—and she was right there in the house with me... it was like a sign from God, you know?" She looked at me helplessly, her eyes swimming. "A sign from God. I had to take her, don't you see? She's mine and she's come home to me and we have to be together. "

"Oh, Ashleigh," I said. How could you argue with a sign from God? "You're fourteen years old. You've got your whole life ahead of you. You can't even get a job without a guardian's permission, and who's going to take care of the baby while you're in school? Ashleigh, you've got to think this through. You tried to do the right thing for your baby once. It's not too late."

She was shaking her head before I finished speaking. Tears were streaming down her face. "Nick is going to get a job. He's sixteen. We're going to go out west, we've got money now—we're going to have money—and I can take care of her. I love her, and I'm her mother, and she's all I've got left, the only family I have. It's going to be fine, we're going to be fine, and you can't take her from me!"

"Ashleigh—"

Behind me the door of the trailer burst open and Nick roared, "Ashleigh, *get in the truck!*"

We both whirled. The baby started screaming. Cisco barked. Melanie exclaimed, "Hey! It's the kid from the drug bust!"

Nick stood at the open door with a cardboard box in his arms and a smell like burning plastic wafting out behind him. His eyes were filled with terror and rage. He shouted at Ashleigh, "She's the one with the damn drug dog! Go! *Go!*"

He plunged down the steps and Ashleigh scrambled to get inside the truck and I saw, incongruently, that the box was filled with baby Jesus figurines. I made a split-second decision. I was close enough to grab Ashleigh or at least the baby. But that would mean leaving Melanie and Cisco, who were on the driver's side of the truck, vulnerable and exposed to Nick. I dashed around the front of the truck toward Melanie just as Nick pushed by with the cardboard box, shouting to Ashleigh, "Get in the truck!"

Another man appeared at the doorway of the trailer and yelled, "Hold it right there, kid, and I mean it! You ain't going nowhere!"

"We had a deal!" Nick shouted at him. He tossed the box in the back of the truck just as I reached Melanie and grabbed Cisco's leash from her hand. She watched with big eyes as Nick wrenched open the driver's door. Ashleigh stood paralyzed, staring at him in horrified disbelief while the baby screamed in her arms and Nick yelled at her, "Get in!"

"You think I don't know what's going on?" The man with rage in his face lunged down the steps of the trailer. It was the man from the trailer park who had asked if Cisco was a drug dog. The man who had been manning the netting stand when we were here the last time. The man they called Dusty, who carried a knife strapped to his belt. "I cut you a deal, trying to be a nice guy, give you a break, the next thing I know you got drug dogs sniffing around here. You narced on me, didn't you kid? Didn't you?"

"Back off, Dusty, I'll run you over, I swear I will!"

Ashleigh was half-in and half-out of the truck, clutching the screaming baby tightly to her chest, her face terrified. The truck engine screeched and roared to life. With a single lunge, Dusty grabbed Ashleigh, his arm beneath her throat and pulled her away from the truck. He had a knife in his hand.

Everything happened in a matter of seconds. The first thing that flashed into my mind was, *That could have been me or Melanie, if I had run the other way when Nick came out.* I began to wonder if there really was such a thing as guardian angels. Cisco started barking excitedly and lunging at the leash. I pulled him back, holding on to Melanie, trying to stay clear of the truck, which had started to roll backwards. Dusty shouted, "I'll off her, I swear I will, and your brat, too! Just like I did her old man when he crossed me! You don't want to mess with me, kid, I got nothing to lose!"

Ashleigh screamed, *"Nick!"* The baby wailed. Nick looked out of the window of the truck, his face stark-white and his eyes wild with fear.

Cisco's barks became high and frantic. Out of the corner of my eye I caught a glimpse of movement from somewhere behind the trailer, and I realized with a shock of dismay and horror what Cisco was barking at. This was the moment. This was the disaster that had been waiting to happen. This was the consequence of my lazy training habits and Cisco's lack of impulse control. He saw Buck behind the trailer, and nothing—not all my strength, not all my prayers, not all the angels in Heaven—could stop him from leaping to the man he loved.

I cried, "Melanie, run!" I jerked mightily on the leash with both hands and tripped over the uneven ground. The leash flew from my hands and Cisco flew from my grasp, racing directly into the path of the oncoming truck. I screamed, *"Cisco!"*

Melanie cried, "Hey!" and scrambled after Cisco. I lurched for her and grabbed only air. Brakes squealed; dirt and gravel flew. I screamed again. Dusty looked from me to the oncoming dog to Nick, but what he did not see was Buck, stepping quietly out from behind the trailer with his gun drawn.

Melanie yelled again, "Hey, Cisco!" and Cisco turned his head in response to her voice. When he did, she turned and ran back toward me. Cisco chased her, just as he might be expected to do, and both of them bounded into my arms. At some point, I was actually able to draw a breath, my heart started beating again, and I heard Buck say, "Drop the knife, Harper."

Nick, with panic in his eyes, slammed the truck into gear and it shot forward. He fought the wheel for control as the truck bounced across the rutted ground toward the dirt road that led down the mountain. But he only made it about twenty yards before a patrol car, with a single blast on its siren, pulled out from the shelter of the tree rows and blocked his way. I could see the cloud of dust that another police car, fast approaching, kicked up in the distance. By the time I looked back at Buck, Dusty was in handcuffs and Buck was saying, "Dusty Harper, you are under arrest for the murder of Earl Lewis, and for manufacturing and trafficking in controlled substances. You have the right to remain silent…"

"Holy cow," Melanie said, big eyed. "It's a real drug bust!"

My knees started to turn to jelly. I sank slowly to the ground, one arm around Melanie, the other around Cisco. "Your dad," I managed, my whole body shaking, "is going to kill me."

***

Within minutes, the mountaintop was swarming with police cars. Nick was in one, Dusty was in another, and Ashleigh was sobbing in a third. Deputies moved in and out of the trailer, removing equipment and product. Peggy Miller arrived in an

SUV with Ruth and Jack Holloway. The car had barely stopped moving before Ruth tumbled out, dressed only in jeans and a sweater with house slippers on her bare feet. Her expression was frantic and she looked neither right nor left but ran straight for the sound of the crying baby. Almost as soon as the baby was transferred to her arms, the wails diminished into weary, gurgling whimpers.

Melanie took it all in with confident, eager absorption. "It's a meth lab," she informed me. "We should have figured. Meth labs account for up to twenty percent of the gross income in rural populations. Lucky it didn't blow up," she added matter-of-factly. "We'd all be ka-powy."

Once again, she left me without anything at all to say.

Buck came over to me, greeting us with a pleasant nod and a tip of his hat. "Afternoon, ladies," he said, glancing around. "Shopping for a Christmas tree?"

"What are you doing here?" I demanded hoarsely. "You couldn't have gotten here this fast. I only called five minutes ago." My throat was still dry, and every time I thought about Cisco and Melanie dashing into the path of that truck my hands started to shake again. To hide it, I kept them tightly wound around Cisco's leash, which did not discourage him from making anxious, happy sounds in his throat and trying to leap up on Buck.

"I'm a cop, "he reminded me, rubbing Cisco's ears. "Solving crimes is kind of what I do."

Then he turned his smile on Melanie. "So, princess. We've got to see what we can do about getting you some kind of commendation. You not only saved Cisco's life, but Ashleigh's too. If you hadn't distracted the bad guy while I snuck up on him, there's no telling what he might have done. How did you know to do that, anyway?"

Melanie's eyes were glowing and her cheeks were bright pink with pride, but she admitted, "Raine taught me. I didn't mean to save anybody. I just didn't want Cisco to run away. The last time we had to chase him, it was really hard."

I was starting to like that kid. A lot.

Buck's eyes crinkled with a grin. "Well, it was quick thinking, anyway. You were right about something else, too—using those baby Jesus figurines to transport drugs. The ones we found at Nick's house just hadn't been used yet."

"Wow," Melanie said, impressed with herself.

Buck added to me in a slightly lower tone, "Or Nick might have gotten the idea from her—we're not too clear on that one yet. The photo you sent me this morning," he went on. "It was Ashleigh in the background, all right—but she was standing by a Walt's Christmas Tree Farm truck. They're the ones who delivered the town tree that afternoon, and it turns out Dusty was driving. We had already figured him for Lewis's partner in the burglary ring, and it just seemed like too much of a coincidence – he's the last one to see Ashleigh's father alive, then he's right there with her, practically in the same picture. So we came up here to ask a few more questions. Turns out it was just a coincidence, but when I saw your car...well, our timing was pretty good, huh?"

I swallowed hard. "So—it was just an accident you were here? And if you hadn't been..." I couldn't think about what might have happened, or almost certainly would have happened, if he hadn't been. I started to get shaky again. "We need to go," I said. "Can we go now?"

Buck held up a detaining finger and turned to Melanie. "Princess Melanie," he said soberly, "would you be good enough to look after this fine steed here while I have a word with Miss Raine?"

She giggled and took Cisco's leash. "You're funny."

"Thank you," he replied. "I try."

Buck touched my arm and we walked a few steps away. I kept Melanie and Cisco in my peripheral vision. "Really, Buck," I said. "I'm late. We haven't even had lunch."

He said, "It looks like Earl was killed when he found out about the meth lab and tried to horn in on Dusty's profits. There are blood stains on the floor inside the trailer that I'm pretty sure we'll find out belonged to Lewis. And Nick, the stupid kid, was just trying to do the right thing and take care of his girl. His friend, Dave, put him on to the drug operation, and Dusty promised him a thousand dollars to drive those figurines filled with crystal meth to Texas."

I shook my head in disbelief, thinking about Nick dumping a box of puppies by my mailbox because he knew if he didn't they would be drowned. Trying to do the right thing. "That's crazy," I said, "and sad, and infuriating."

Buck nodded. "You're talking about a drunk, two teenagers, and a guy who used more of his product than he sold. I guess the only surprise here is that no more than one person got killed."

I was trying not to think about that. "What about Ashleigh?"

"She'll be charged with child endangerment. What happens after that is up to the court."

I looked toward the police car where Ashleigh was sitting and crying, and I was overwhelmed with sadness. "She's only a few years older than Melanie."

"You know how it is, Raine. All these kids want is to be loved, and they go looking for it in the wrong place. At least the baby's okay."

I sighed. "At least." I turned to go back to Melanie. "We need to head back."

He touched my arm, detaining me. He said, "I owe you an apology."

I looked at him, and his expression was tight and uncomfortable, the way it always was when he knew he was wrong and didn't like to admit it. My attention quickened.

"About the Christmas party," he said quietly. He avoided my eyes. "I should have told you Wyn was coming. I don't know what I was thinking."

Given my choice of every topic known to man, perhaps the only conversation I would have liked to have had less was the one in which I explained to Melanie's father that I had just taken his daughter to a meth lab and exposed her to a killer. I started to walk away.

He said, "Do you know what happens to a man when he doesn't have a wife around to tell him when he's acting like a jackass?"

Reluctantly, I turned to look at him. "He acts like a jackass?"

"Right."

We looked at each other for another long moment. I said, "So who told you that you had acted like a jackass this time?"

He didn't answer, but he didn't have to. Well, what had expected?

Like I said, I've always liked Wyn.

After a moment I said, "So. Are you having Christmas dinner at her house?"

He nodded, slowly. "Yeah." And he held my gaze. There was no apology there.

In another moment I managed a smile. "Well. I guess I won't see you before then, so Merry Christmas."

"Merry Christmas, Raine."

I had walked a few steps away before he said, "Hey."

I looked back.

"You'll always be my family," he said.

I walked back to Melanie, and took Cisco's leash. My eyes were stinging, but I smiled as I put my arm around her shoulders. "Come on," I said, and gave her a little squeeze. "Let's get you home. We've got some explaining to do."

SEVENTEEN

S ometimes I think there really are such things as Christmas miracles. Not only was Miles not mad at me, he actually thanked me for keeping Melanie safe. And when she told him the story—with the inimitable drama to which she was prone—he made her feel every bit the hero that she insisted she was. I thought he had real potential as a father.

"He said Melanie seemed onboard with the idea of moving in with him," I told Sonny a couple of days later. "I think she was afraid all along she would have to move to Brazil. Moving to Atlanta must seem like a pretty good trade."

"Still," Sonny said, "losing a mother can't be easy."

I thought about Ashleigh and the infant who, it now appeared, had a chance at a wonderful life because she had given her up. "It depends on the mother, I guess."

Sonny had stopped by to leave a spare key to her house, and I had promised to catch her up on all the news before she left for the winter. We shared one of Aunt Mart's coffee cakes and exchanged gifts for the dogs: I had a box of organic gingerbread dog cookies I had ordered online for Mystery and Hero, and she brought individually wrapped cheese-stuffed marrow bones for each of my dogs, which they munched on enthusiastically while we talked.

Sonny took another sip of her coffee, reading my mind. "So, I saw Mark James at a Christmas party last night." Mark James was our county prosecutor. "He's not going to try Nick as an adult."

I released a breath of relief. "That's good. I don't think he's a bad kid at heart. He just got caught up in a bad situation, and tried to do the best he could to make it right. Aunt Mart said social services was finally able to contact Ashleigh's aunt in Ohio and they're taking her in. They've even got her enrolled in school right after Christmas. The Holloways are at the top of the adoption list for baby Hope, and meanwhile they're fostering her. Aunt Mart said they had painted the nursery like a scene out of a fairy tale, and the church has given them so many baby showers that they've started rewrapping the gifts and sending them to children's homes for the holidays."

"It kind of makes you believe in the magic of Christmas," she said.

"Speaking of Magic..." I told her the story of Magic, Mischief, and the mysterious Christmas decorating caper, and she laughed out loud with delight.

"So it was Magic all along," she practically chortled. "Did I call it or not? Mischief said she was framed."

I may have mentioned that Sonny is a world-class attorney. It did not, however, surprise me as much as you might think that she was more interested in the mystery of the dogs than in the major crime that had taken place in our small community in the past few days.

"Mischief," I replied with a small frown, "still has a lot of explaining to do. And so does Magic. But what's funny is that since we caught them on tape they've both been perfect angels. No more incidents."

Sonny laughed. "I guess they got their point across—whatever it was, of course."

"I guess. As for Cisco," I added, and the culprit's eyes lifted from his stuffed marrow bone long enough to give me a baleful look, "that's the last time my life will ever flash before my eyes because he doesn't know the meaning of 'stay.' I think you were right," I admitted. "First I had Hero living here, then it was the puppies, and Cisco was always pushed to the background. So the first thing after Christmas we're starting a training program that will turn him into the star he already thinks he is. Before the year is out, there won't be a blue ribbon in the state that doesn't have his name on it."

Sonny grinned. "Cisco says every blue ribbon in the state *already* has his name on it. You just don't know it yet."

She finished her coffee and reached for the pronged cane that helped her keep her balance on bad days. "Well, I've got a long drive ahead. Thanks for being my back-up with the house." She stopped and looked at me with sudden query, her expression filled with concern. "It just occurred to me. Are you going to be alone for Christmas?"

I gave her a casual, dismissing wave. "Don't be silly. I'm going to have a great Christmas." I was going to be alone for Christmas.

"Because with Maude in Florida and your aunt and uncle on the cruise...."

Cisco interrupted with a single *woof* and looked up from his bone with ears pricked and eyes pointed toward the window. A moment later I saw a glint of sunlight reflected on the highly waxed surface of a black town car as it pulled into the circular drive in front of my house. Mischief and Magic grabbed their bones and scurried toward the front door. Cisco barked again, decided he had done his duty and turned back to his bone with renewed enthusiasm.

When I opened the door, a neatly groomed man in a Burberry overcoat stood there with a briefcase, looking cold and uncomfortable, his collar turned up against the wind. I glanced over his shoulder at the expensive car parked in my driveway and then back at him. He was definitely a stranger.

"Miss Stockton?"

I nodded.

"My name is Jason Wells." He handed me a card from his pocket. "I've been trying to get in touch with you for over a week. I left several messages and even stopped by a couple of times. It's important that I speak with you. "

I glanced at the card and gradually made the connection with the multiple telephone messages he had left. "You are persistent," I said, and offered the card back to him, "but I'm not interested. I have all the insurance I can afford."

"This is not about insurance," he assured me. A blast of wind made the Christmas wreath that was hung on the porch column swing, and he hunched his shoulders against it, glancing down at the two dogs by my side. "Do you think we could talk inside? It's about Esther Kelp."

I felt a sinking in my stomach, and I opened the door wider to admit him. "Oh, no. Is she dead?"

"She was fine the last time I spoke with her," he said as he stepped inside. "She's living with her grandson in California. She's the one who gave me your name. If you prefer, of course, we can do this at your attorney's office, but..." He smiled, "It's almost Christmas, and I have children back in Boston, and the sooner we can get this wrapped up the happier I'll be."

I was more confused than ever and a little alarmed. "Am I in some kind of trouble?"

Sonny came up behind me. "Is everything okay, Raine?"

"He says I need an attorney."

I could sense all of Sonny's lawyerly instincts switch on, and she turned her gaze on the stranger. "I'm Miss Stockton's attorney. What's this all about?"

"Please," said Mr. Wells, "I can explain everything if we can just sit down a minute."

I glanced at Sonny, gave a small shrug, and led the way back into the living room, where there was a cheery fire. Cisco, sprawled out in front of the Christmas tree with his bone, glanced up and swished his tail in greeting, but could not be bothered further. Mischief and Magic flopped down beside him.

When we were settled, Mr. Wells got right to the point. "I represent the estate of John F. Kennedy," he said without preamble, and my eyes widened. "I understand Mrs. Kelp gave you some items of historical significance that the family would very much like to have for their private collection. I'm prepared to offer you a significant sum for their return."

I looked at Sonny, but she seemed as confused as I was. I looked back at Mr. Wells. "The shoes?" I said.

Now he looked confused. "What shoes?"

"The ones Miss Esther gave me. She said she had danced with Jack Kennedy in them."

He frowned a little. "Miss Stockton, I'm not here about shoes. I understood you were in possession of a number of letters that were written to Mrs. Kelp by—well, as I said, they are of considerable historical significance. You *do* have them, don't you?"

Sonny said, "Letters?" She looked at me. "You never said anything about letters."

"There was an envelope of letters and old postcards in the bottom of the shoe box that Mischief—I mean Magic—kept dragging around. Magic is my dog," I explained to Mr. Wells, and I thought his face actually lost a little color.

"You don't mean—your dog didn't–?"

"Oh no, they're fine," I assured him. "My dogs don't destroy things. Most of the time. I was going to send the letters back to Miss Esther, but I haven't had time to find her new address."

He released a cautious breath. "May I see them?"

I went to the dining room, where I had stored the empty boxes of Christmas decorations, and found the shoe box tucked inside one of them. I brought the manila envelope back into the living room and watched in absolute astonishment as Jason Wells put on a pair of white gloves before removing the contents and then, very carefully, unfolding and scanning the letters that were inside. A smile spread over his face as he read. I never got to see what they said. Or who they were from.

The only sound was the munching of dog bones for the longest time. He refolded and replaced the letters in their original envelopes with the greatest of care and then placed the envelopes in a plastic bag that he took from his briefcase. From the same briefcase he took out a sheaf of legal-sized papers, on top of which was clipped a check. The check he passed to me. The papers he passed to Sonny. "This is what we are prepared to offer for the letters," he said. To Sonny he added, "These are the conditions of the sale."

I stared at the numbers on the check. The last time I had seen that many of them I had been in a bank, signing loan papers. I looked up at him. "Is this a joke?"

"I assure you, it is not."

I looked at Sonny, who had her glasses on and was intently scrutinizing the document she had been handed. "Is this a joke?"

She murmured, without looking up, "Apparently not."

I looked again at the check. It was enough to complete the renovations on my building, *and* make up for the business we had lost while being closed. It was more than enough.

Mr. Wells added, "You understand we are only interested in the letters. But as an estate appraiser, I have to tell you many of the postcards are quite collectible—some are worth thousands. They are yours to do with as you please, of course."

"Come on," I said, starting to grin as I glanced down at the postcards spilling from the envelope. "Who put you up to this?"

Sonny flipped the last page of the contract and removed her glasses. "It looks authentic to me.

There's even a signed letter of transfer from Mrs. Kelp, giving you full ownership of everything that was in that envelope."

Once again, I stared at her, my head reeling. "But—but if this stuff really is that valuable, she shouldn't have given it to me. This belongs to her family, her grandson. I'm sure they could use it for her care."

Mr. Wells chuckled. "Miss Stockton, do you know who her grandson is?"

I shook my head.

"Believe me, he doesn't need the money. Here, ask her for yourself." He took another paper from his briefcase upon which was written a telephone number with an unfamiliar area code. "Call her."

Far away in California my telephone call was answered by a man who identified himself as Miss Esther's grandson. When he told me his name, I almost dropped the phone. His last movie had grossed 82 million dollars on opening weekend.

Eventually I managed to gather my wits enough to ask, "Did you—um, did you happened to buy the rights to Miss Esther's life story for a movie?"

He chuckled. "I've been trying to get Gran to let me make that movie for over ten years. We settled the deal the day after she got out here. It's going to be huge. Huge."

We chatted for a few more minutes—he was a really nice man—and he assured me he had copies of the letters and was more than happy to let the originals go to the estate. Then he transferred me to Esther's cottage and she was delighted to hear from me. She told me about the orange tree that grew outside her window and having lunch at Spago and oh, yes, the movie her grandson was making of her life. I tried to thank her for the enormity of her gift but she was dismissive. "I knew you'd put it to good use," she said. "Lord knows, it's been a curse and a blessing all my life, and I'm glad to know I'm only passing on the blessing."

Finally I got up the courage to ask her the big question. "Did you really work for the CIA?"

Her laugh was light and musical and took me back, across the miles, to all the good times and good stories we had shared together. "Now, honey, you're just going to have to watch my movie, aren't you? You give that sweet Cisco a hug, you hear? And have a merry Christmas."

I was beginning to think I would.

The crew that Miles loaned me did not completely get my building finished before Christmas, but almost. The indoor runs were completed, the training room needed only paint, and the grooming room was lacking only the tubs. Cisco's big Christmas present— the one I could not wait to try out—was the new indoor agility training ring, complete with recycled rubber flooring and brand new, state-of-the-art, solid-steel agility equipment. Beginning first thing

Christmas morning, Cisco and I were going to start training for the national championship. After all, if I could discover a fortune in a fifty-year-old box of shoes, anything was possible.

In my new, bright yellow and primary blue office—two of the easiest colors for dogs to see, by the way—there was a framed vintage postcard of Lassie doing her famous wave. All of the other post cards had gone into the safety deposit box with my mother's jewelry and awaited appraisal.

On Christmas Eve morning, Miles and Melanie stopped by for brunch on their way to Myrtle Beach. Aunt Mart had dropped off Majesty the night before, and she greeted the company in a red velvet, jingle bell collar with her classic bouncing collie bark. Melanie placed a huge, cellophane wrapped basket filled with dog toys, dog biscuits and gourmet dog cookies underneath the Christmas tree, and told me how she had hand-picked each treat from the pet store in Asheville. All of the dogs, of course, fixated upon the basket, which made her giggle with delight. The best thing about my dogs is that they know how to appreciate a gift when it's offered.

She had chosen a darling little gift pack of red-and-white plush toys for the orphaned puppy that even I had begun to call Pepper. It was hard to see the disappointment on Melanie's face when she ran to the kitchen only to see that the ex-pen—and the puppy—were gone, but when I explained to her that the puppy had found a new home with a great family, she took it bravely. "Maybe I can mail this to her," she said, gazing down sadly at the gaily wrapped Christmas package. I assured her that she could, and she made an effort to pretend that was okay.

"I guess I'll be having a new home too," she added with exaggerated casualness, and I met Miles's eyes over her head with a smile in my own. "Right after Christmas, I'm going to start looking at schools in Atlanta. So these new people, do they have a fenced yard?"

I promised her they did.

"Who's their vet?"

I told her they weren't from around here.

"But they signed her up for puppy classes, right?"

"Oh, yes, I made sure of that. Do you want to help me slice this fruit?"

Miles of course wanted to inspect the work on the kennel and came back with a punch list that was even longer than the original work order. "Be sure they come back and touch up the paint when they fix that trim," he told me. "Fast work doesn't excuse sloppy work. You're paying for the finished job. Make sure it's done right before you sign that check."

I gave him a look of exaggerated forbearance. "That's right," I told him. "I'm paying for it."

He grinned. "Boundaries, right?"

"Right."

Miles is usually the cook when we get together, for obvious reasons, but I wanted a chance to show off, and even he had to admit my pancakes were delicious.

Both he and Melanie had seconds. "So now we know you can cook breakfast," he said, eyes twinkling. "We have to find some way to take advantage of that."

I settled back in my chair, cradling my coffee cup against my chest, smiling at him in an extraordinarily silly way. "You're in an awfully good mood."

"Why shouldn't I be? It's Christmas. Are you sure you won't change your mind and come to the beach with us?"

"Don't be silly, Miles. I have the dogs."

"Yeah, Dad," Melanie chimed in, "she can't leave the dogs." Then she said, "These people, where do they live?"

For a moment I didn't know what she was talking about. I was still looking at Miles, and fantasizing, however absurdly, about the beach. I said, "Um... somewhere outside of Atlanta I think."

Her eyes lit up. "Maybe I could do a follow-up visit for you! I'm good at filling out reports." Her expression became tinged with anxiety. "I mean, if you think I should. If that would be okay."

I met Miles's eyes across the table. Mine were saying, *I'm crazy about this kid*. I don't know what his were saying. I'm not that good at reading men. But whatever it was, it gave me a funny, happy feeling in the pit of my stomach. I turned to Melanie, smiling. "That sounds great, Melanie."

Melanie looked pleased, and turned to her father. "You know, Dad," she said seriously, "I've been thinking I might have a career in law enforcement. Maybe training drug dogs."

Miles said, "I think you'd probably be great at that. However, I want to go on record as saying I do not support any career that puts my daughter in the line of gunfire."

Melanie sipped her juice and considered that. "I don't think dog trainers get shot at much."

Boy, did I have a few stories to relate on that subject. But for once I kept my mouth shut, and I studiously avoided Miles's gaze.

Miles wasn't fooled though. "I read the article in the paper yesterday," he said. "It didn't say anything about charging the owner of the tree farm."

"That's the weird thing," I said. "The meth lab wasn't on Walt's property, and Uncle Roe says he didn't have any idea what was going in that trailer. Apparently Dusty—and Nick, for that matter—could drive up to it on a dirt road from the highway."

"Hmm." He sipped his coffee. "It also said that that the hostages were held at knifepoint. I don't think you mentioned that."

I widened my eyes innocently. "Didn't I?"

He looked as though he wanted to say more, but Melanie interrupted with, "Can the dogs open their present now?"

Miles looked at me steadily for another moment then surprised me. "I think that's a great idea," he agreed, setting down his cup. "Let's have presents."

We left the breakfast dishes on the table and trooped to the living room with excited dog claws clicking on the wood floors behind us. The Christmas tree was alight with multi-colored lights, and four stockings, already plump with the treats people had been bringing by all week, hung over the fireplace. Miles stirred up the fire while I folded back the protective fence from the tree and Melanie dragged out the big basket of treats. Absolute chaos ensued, of course, and Miles and I plopped ourselves down on the floor in the middle of it, laughing and brushing away swiping tails and wriggling furry bodies and slobbery kisses. Like any other pet owner, I reveled in seeing my dogs happy, and Christmas was a once-a-year celebration, so I allowed them to gobble far more dog cookies than was probably wise. Eventually, though, I had to call an end to the bacchanal and confiscate the Basket of Endless Dog Treats. I allowed Melanie to pick one toy for each dog and laughed until my face hurt, watching them roll and dash and dart and play bow and toss their toys in the air.

"Good job, Melanie," I declared. "You are now officially the best dog-Christmas-present-giver ever."

She glowed under my praise and chose a peanut butter flavored ball to toss for Majesty. She laughed out loud when Majesty caught it in midair.

Miles, watching his daughter, didn't seem to be able to stop smiling. Then he surprised me by reaching under the Christmas tree and bringing out a medium-sized flat box wrapped in gold foil with a big silvery-blue bow. "Merry Christmas," he said, and handed it to me.

Now, I have to say, no one loves presents more than I do—except, perhaps, Cisco. But I took the gift with a mixture of excitement and dismay. "Miles," I said, "we had an agreement. We weren't going to exchange gifts."

He shrugged. "I have trouble with boundaries."

He sat with his arm propped up on one upraised knee and his index finger partially obscuring his mouth, but his eyes were brimming with quiet amusement. I had to grin back. "You're incorrigible."

"So I've been told."

Melanie stopped tossing the ball and watched me as I unwrapped the gift. I was more than a little excited as I peeled away the foil and opened the box. "Oh," I said, staring at the contents. "It's a phone."

"Not just any phone," Miles pointed out. "The very latest in smartphone technology. It's got a camera with video chat, a GPS, and a satellite sim chip that will allow you to call anywhere in the world. All powered up and ready to use." He added, "My number is programmed in. Number one."

Melanie added, "Mine is number two. I got one just like it."

I had to smile. "Thanks. It's really great." I removed the device carefully from its foam holder. "Really…useful."

"You don't like it," Miles said. I could see he was trying to feign disappointment. "I should have gone with the fruit-of-the-month."

"I told you she wouldn't," Melanie said. "Girls like romantic things. And she's a girl."

"No, really," I said. "It's great, really. It's just…"

"Too expensive?" suggested Miles. "I guess it's a good thing I didn't go with my first impulse, then." I could see Melanie's eyes, bright and eager with a secret, watching as he reached into his pocket and brought out a small, distinctive blue box. He offered it to me, palm up. "Jewelry."

My breath actually stopped. I'd never had anything from Tiffany's, not ever. I took the box from him and opened it reverently. Inside was a pair of sterling silver, bone-shaped earrings, each one studded with a small diamond.

I squealed out loud with delight and Melanie clapped her hands, laughing. Miles's eyes danced. I wanted to fling myself into his lap and kiss him hard on the mouth, but, aware of the presence of children and dogs, I managed to restrain myself. I couldn't stop beaming, though, as I put on the earrings, gave my head a little toss, and said, "Good choice. You've got real possibilities, you know that?"

He inclined his head modestly toward Melanie. "Thank you. But I had expert advice."

She grinned at him and held her hand up for a high five. He slapped her hand, and I laughed, reaching under the tree for another small package. "Okay, my turn," I said. I presented the package to Melanie. "Just a little something to thank you for all your help," I said casually. "You know, with the puppies."

Miles rose and quietly left the room. I watched, barely able to contain my excitement, as Melanie unwrapped the package and opened the box. Her expression turned to absolute bewilderment as she gazed at the contents. Inside, nestled on a bed of cotton batting, was a peppermint-striped collar and leash.

Behind her, Miles said, "Merry Christmas, sweetheart." He set the small fuzzy puppy on the floor.

Melanie gasped, "Pepper!"

The puppy, who had been patiently waiting in my newly decorated kennel office, raced to her, comically clumsy as it slipped and slid on the hardwood floor. I had even fastened a red-and-white-striped bow around her neck, which I was glad to see was not too much the worse for wear. Melanie tumbled toward her puppy, and I have to admit I wiped moisture from my eyes as I watched the reunion. She swept the puppy up and covered it with kisses and the puppy reciprocated, and then my dogs had to get in on the act, milling around and mugging for attention until I called them back to my side with fresh treats from their holiday basket.

I stood beside Miles and we watched as Melanie fitted the pup with her new collar and leash. Her face was radiant. "Good decision," I murmured.

He tried to look nonchalant, but I could tell his daughter's pleasure thrilled him as much as it did me.

"You're probably right," he said, "It will help with the adjustment. Of course..." And he looked at me darkly, "you know who's going to get stuck taking care of it while she's in school."

"It will build character," I told him.

Melanie suddenly rushed to him and flung her arms around his knees. "Dad, thank you, thank you! I love you so much! It's the best Christmas ever!"

Miles knelt down and hugged his daughter and the puppy jumped up on both of them, as though she wanted to share in the embrace. This time, I was pushing wetness from my eyes with both hands.

"Okay, sweetie," Miles said, giving her a kiss. "Take the pup outside for a walk before we get in the car. It's a long ride to Grandma's."

Melanie hurried outside with the puppy, and I helped Miles gather up all the equipment they would need for the trip—the travel crate, premium puppy food, dishes, portable play pen and chew toys that he had ordered online and had delivered to the kennel address so that Melanie wouldn't suspect. "It's worse than traveling with a baby," he complained, looking at the pile beside the door.

I grinned. "Fortunately, you're a good dad."

A corner of his lips quirked dryly. "Remains to be seen." Then he looked at me, and something in his eyes made my heart beat faster. "Thanks, Raine," he said. "I wish I didn't have to leave."

I said, "I wish you didn't have to, either." And I meant it.

Miles said, "I can find a place for you on the beach that would take dogs. There's no point in being alone at Christmas."

I smiled broadly and gestured toward the Christmas tree. A collie, a golden retriever, and two Australian shepherds were settled around it in an eerily accurate reproduction of the dogs in my porcelain Nativity scene, contentedly munching their bones. Four velvet stockings were overflowing. And tomorrow Cisco and I began training in our brand new agility room.

I said simply, "I'm not going to be alone."

His eyes softened, and he seemed to understand. "Melanie gets a school holiday in a few weeks. We'll be back."

I had to smile. "Look at you, counting school holidays already."

He just stood there, smiling back.

Then he turned and started to pull on his coat. "Well, I guess we'd better get started if we want to get there before dark. If I have to stop every two hours to let the puppy out the drive is going to take twice as long. I'll call you tonight. Meanwhile ..."

"Hey, dummy," I said.

He turned and looked at me.

I said, "I chose one."

I stood underneath the arch of the foyer, and when I cast my eyes meaningfully upward toward the mistletoe that hung overhead the puzzlement on his face faded into a slow and confident smile. He slipped his coat off his arms and tossed it aside. He came toward me, holding my eyes. He stood close. He drew me into his arms. He smelled wonderful.

And then he kissed me.

Oh, my. Best Christmas ever.

Other Books in the Raine Stockton Dog Mystery Series

SMOKY MOUNTAIN TRACKS

A child has been kidnapped and abandoned in the mountain wilderness. Her only hope is Raine Stockton and her young, untried tracking dog Cisco...

RAPID FIRE

Raine and Cisco are brought in by the FBI to track a terrorist ...a terrorist who just happens to be Raine's old boyfriend.

GUN SHY

Raine rescues a traumatized service dog, and soon begins to suspect he is the only witness to a murder.

BONE YARD

Cisco digs up human remains in Raine's back yard, and mayhem ensues. Could this be evidence of a serial killer, a long-unsolved mass murder, or something even more sinister... and closer to home?

Learn more about Donna and her dogs at
www.dogdazejournal.blogspot.com

More by This Author

RENEGADE by Donna Boyd

The Long- Awaited Third Installment in the Devoncroix Dynasty

Emory Hilliford, a quiet anthropology professor, is drugged, held captive and interrogated by a mysterious stranger who wants only one thing: the truth about an ancient race of beings known as the lupinotuum, half man/half wolf, who have walked among humans for centuries. Once they ruled the tundra, now they rule Wall Street. Once they fought with teeth and claws, now they fight with wealth and power. And Emory Hilliford, an orphan who was raised by a family of sophisticated, influential lupinotuum in twentieth century Venice, is uniquely positioned to chronicle their culture, their history, and their secrets.

Unknown to all but a select few, Emory has also been carefully groomed to play a crucial role in history, one that could have deadly consequences for his own race, and theirs. Now forced to tell his story, Emory must decide how much of the truth he can afford to reveal, and what secrets he will take to his grave... because his own time is running out.

From the ancient legends of Greece and Rome to the mysteries of the Dark Ages and the glitter of modern day New York, RENEGADE is a sweeping saga of passion and betrayal, sacrifice and destiny, that will consume your days and haunt your nights long after the last page is turned.

Heart-pounding suspense by Donna Ball

NIGHT FLIGHT

She's an innocent woman who knows too much. Now she's fleeing through the night without a weapon and without a phone, and her only hope for survival is a cop who's willing to risk his badge—and his life—to save her.

SANCTUARY

They came to the peaceful, untouched mountain wilderness of Eastern Tennessee seeking an escape from the madness of modern life. But when they built their luxury homes in the heart of virgin forest they did not realize that something was there before them... something ancient and horrible; something that will make them believe that monsters are real.

EXPOSURE

Everyone has secrets, but when talk show host Jessamine's Cray's stalker begins to use her past to terrorize her, no one is safe ... not her family, her friends, her coworkers, and especially not Jess herself.

Romance Revisited by Donna Ball

MATCHMAKER, MATCHMAKER

He was a cowboy looking for a wife. She was a lady specializing in brides. They were made for each other... They just didn't know it yet.

A MAN AROUND THE HOUSE

He was the answer to a busy working woman's dreams. But was he too good to be true?

FOR KEEPS

He's an animal trainer who lives by one rule: never get attached. She's a social worker who knows all too well the price of getting involved. It may take an entire menagerie to bring them together, but eventually they both must learn that sometimes it's for keeps.

STEALING SAVANNAH

He was a reformed jewel thief now turned security expert and her job depended on his expertise. But could he be trusted not to steal the most valuable jewel of all-- her heart?

UNDER COVER

She's working on the biggest case of her life, and her cover has already been blown-- by the very man she's investigating. Now they must work together to solve an even bigger mystery-- their future together.

THE STORMRIDERS

They were thunder and lightning when they were married, and their divorce has been no less turbulent. But trapped together during a deadly blizzard with the lives of an entire community depending on them, they discover what's really important, and that some storms are worth riding out.

INTERLUDE

Sometimes a chance encounter is over in a moment, and sometimes it can last a lifetime.

CAST ADRIFT

She was a marine biologist on short deadline to find a very important dolphin, with no time to waste on romance. He was a sailor who knew there could only be one captain on his ship-- himself. But two weeks at sea together could change everything...

*The puppy training tips in this book were taken from **Ten Things Your Puppy Needs to Know To be A Great Dog** by D.A.Ball, available through the same retailer where you purchased this book.*

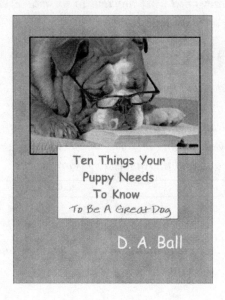

Ten Things Your
Puppy Needs
To Know
To Be A Great Dog

D. A. Ball

ABOUT THE AUTHOR....

Donna Ball is the author of over a hundred novels under several different pseudonyms in a variety of genres that include romance, mystery, suspense, paranormal, western adventure, historical and women's fiction. Recent popular series include the Ladybug Farm series by Berkley Books and the Raine Stockton Dog Mystery series. Donna is an avid dog lover and her dogs have won numerous titles for agility, obedience and canine musical freestyle. She lives in a restored Victorian Barn in the heart of the Blue Ridge mountains with a variety of four-footed companions. You can contact her at www.donnaball.net.